# "Surrendering Her Heart"
## A Lesbian Romance

Jenny Bloom

This book is intended for Adults (ages 18+) only. The contents may be offensive to some readers. It may contain graphic language, explicit sexual content, and adult situations. May contain scenes of unprotected sex. Please do not read this book if you are offended by content as mentioned above or if you are under the age of 18. Please educate yourself on safe sex practices before making potentially life-changing decisions about sex in real life.

This story is a work of fiction. Names, characters, businesses, places, events and incidents are the products of the author's imagination or used in a fictitious manner & are not to be construed as real. Any resemblance to actual persons, living or dead, or actual events is purely coincidental. Products or brand names mentioned are trademarks of their respective holders or companies. The cover uses licensed images & are shown for illustrative purposes only. Any person(s) that may be depicted on the cover are simply models.

Edition v1.00 (2020.04.07)
www.JennyBloomAuthor.com

Special thanks to the following volunteer readers who helped with proofreading: Jenn, RB, Naomi W., and those who assisted but wished to be anonymous. Thank you so much for your support.

# Chapter One

*They leave the parking lot, but they don't head back for Kayla Masterson's house. Sheila Farris doesn't know where they're going until she smells the ocean breeze when she rolls down the window.*

*"I like to escape from reality a lot. One minute I could be at the club and the next here at the ocean where it's nice and quiet." Kayla doesn't take her eyes off the road until she's completely parked.*

*Shutting off the car and leaving the headlights on, Kayla grins at Sheila and gets out of the car. Sheila laughs at her when she watches her run down to the water. Then she watches her kick up the sand under her bare feet.*

*"Come on! Get out here!" Kayla shouts to her. Sheila gets out of the car the second she hears her voice.*

*Sheila runs down to the sand. Then, they run into the ocean together.*

*"This is crazy, do you know that?" Sheila hollers out to Kayla above the noise of the surf.*

*"It's what I like to do. I like to have a lot of fun. I work a lot, but when I let loose, I let loose." Kayla giggles, going waist-deep into the ocean before running back out.*

*She feels the coolness on her skin. Her dress sticks to her. At that moment, she knows the memory will be with her for the rest of her life.*

*"We didn't even bring extra clothes," Sheila tells her, knowing that they're going to get the seats wet in the car.*

*"You always live by the rules. For once, just let it all go. Let yourself go." Kayla throws her head back and laughs as they race to the car.*

*Sheila can't remember the last time she had so much fun with anyone. She'd never met anyone like Kayla. She is a woman who doesn't have to worry about anything. It truly excites Sheila, knowing Kayla wants to be with her.*

*Kayla turns the heat on before she even bothers leaving the ocean. They're both shivering, teeth chattering.*

*"This was a great night. I don't care. It's one for the books." Sheila giggles, feeling her teeth click against each other.*

*"Same, I haven't done anything like this in a very long time. Ted was just too boring. He didn't like to take risks. He also always lives by the rules. The other one didn't even want to be seen in public with me." Kayla shakes off the horrible feeling of that time.*

*"I think that anyone would be lucky to have you by their side," Sheila tells her, taking her hand and holding it tightly.*

*"Me too," Kayla tells her. They go into another fit of giggles as if they're high school kids. Sheila laughs until her sides hurt, and her lungs ache.*

*"Are you ready to go back to the house?" Kayla asks when the car is nice and heated.*

*"Yes. I'm ready to call it a night." Sheila nods her head. Kayla pulls out of the parking lot.*

*By the time they get back to the house, it's almost one in the morning. They climb the stairs and get into something dryer.*

"Where are you going?" Kayla asks as she watches Sheila leave the bathroom and head down the hall.

"I thought that you might want some space. Some time for yourself." Sheila shrugs her shoulders.

"If I wanted space, I would tell you. Unless you don't want to share my bed tonight." Kayla grins at her.

Sheila loves how hazel her eyes are. The twinkle in them shows Sheila that Kayla doesn't want to call it a night. She doesn't want the night to end at all.

She goes into the bedroom and lays on the other side of the bed. Pulling the blanket back and feeling her body relax.

"Tonight was nice. Thanks for going out with me. I honestly didn't think that you would, you surprised me." Kayla nods her head, looking over at her.

"You thought I was going to cancel on you?" Sheila asks, a little offended by the idea.

"Well, after today, I didn't think that you would have the energy to go." Kayla winks at her, and Sheila feels her heart skip a beat.

These are the moments Sheila wants to hold Kayla closer to her. If she were in her room, Kayla would have been thinking about how great the day had been. The ups and the downs.

"Are you going to go back to the working momma routine when Alex comes home? I mean hiding behind the doors and not coming out even for dinner?" Sheila asks her.

"I don't know. I do like the fun that we're having right now. I know that I have to balance my work. I can't just be a ghost the whole time now that you're here. You don't know how hard it was before you showed up. The only time I was able to work was when Alex was in bed. Sometimes that's a struggle as you know for yourself." Kayla points out to her.

Sheila nods her head, looking into Kayla's eyes. She can see that far off look on her face. She knows that she's going to contemplate what's going to happen.

"I do know that I'm going to try my best to start with simple things like joining you guys at dinner. Taking small breaks here and there so that Alex doesn't feel ignored so that you don't feel ignored. There are two people that I need to share my time with now." Kayla giggles. Sheila can hear the emotion in her laughter.

"It's not really that hard. I can help you with that. We'll make a timesheet of when you can take breaks and that sort of thing. The timesheet will show when you're allowed and for how long. Then you're done for the night. Even if you're not finished, there's always another day for it. I used to plan days out, remember?" Sheila asks her.

"That's right. You must miss the daycare center a lot." Kayla tells her, feeling sad for Sheila.

"Not really. I mean, it's not like I got fired. All the workers at the daycare lost their jobs. The owner wasn't keeping up on it. That wasn't our fault. Besides, if I had never left the center, I wouldn't know you or Alex, right?" Sheila shrugs her shoulders.

*"We would've met up one way or another. If it's meant to be, there's always a way." Kayla raises one eyebrow at her.*

*Sheila sees that Kayla believes in magic when it comes to love. No matter how many times she is let down, she still believes that there's magic.*

*"I think that you're right. We might've met up at the grocery store, the ocean. Definitely not the club, though. You wouldn't catch me out at the club unless invited." Sheila laughs at the thought of doing it on her own.*

*"Yeah, I see that. You need to come out of your shell too. If you help me in learning how to take a little time off work, then I'm going to show you how young you really are." Kayla promises her.*

*"I can't wait until Alex comes home. I have to say that I miss chasing him around the house." Sheila stares longingly at the television screen that's not even on.*

***

Sheila thought that it wouldn't be any different than babysitting. At thirty-two, she'd been working at a daycare center until it closed. Now she's here at Kayla's house, taking care of a seven-year-old with golden blond hair and the lightest blue eyes.

She'd only been working there for a week. Yet, Kayla has already attached herself to young Alex, who liked to go on new adventures every day.

Sheila dressed in a white button-down shirt and blue jeans, her long blonde hair being played with by the light breeze that had come across the yard, picking up the fall leaves.

She knew that there wouldn't be too many more times where she'd be able to enjoy the sun before it got cold.

Fall was her favorite season. She didn't like the winter and how cold it could get. Ever hoping that winter wouldn't fall, but it always came.

"What are you doing?" Alex asked, looking up at her, shielding his eyes with his hand to keep the sun out of his eyes.

"Just thinking. Are you ready to go for that walk?" Sheila asked, holding out her hand to him, smiling as he takes it.

"My Mom does the same thing." He shakes his head at her.

Sheila laughs a little as they head down the dirt trail out into the woods. Taking in her surroundings, she is happy to see the leaves changing. She watches as one falls from a branch and realizes that soon the branches will be bare.

Alex lets go of her hand and runs up the path, almost out of sight.

"Don't go too far!" Sheila shouts to him. He stops but doesn't turn around to face her.

Sheila's never known a child to listen as well as he does. She's happy to be a nanny to a child that listens so well.

"I'm going to Dad's this weekend." He points out to her.

"That's what I've heard. I will be here Monday when you return." Sheila tells him, smiling when he lets her catch up to him. Then he runs further down the trail.

Sheila hasn't had a chance to be alone with Kayla, not knowing what she's like and what she does while Alex is gone.

During the week, Kayla works too much. Sheila knows this for a fact. Sometimes it's hard to get Alex to bed because he wants his mother.

Understandably, Sheila knows that.

When she catches up to Alex again, she laughs when she watches him run through the leaves in the open field beyond the trail.

How he throws the leaves up in the air, kicks at them with his shoes, hits them with his hands just to watch them twirl around him again.

"Do you want me to make a pile of them so that you can jump in them?" She asks him when she's close enough.

He nods his head as he throws his head back and laughs at her.

Not a care in the world

Sheila gathers up mounds and mounds of leaves until she has a decent pile. Knowing how deep it is so that he doesn't get hurt when he jumps into them.

There's a boulder in the middle of the field where they're at. Alex climbs it with Sheila behind him, making sure that he doesn't fall.

"On the count of three," Sheila tells him.

He looks down at the pile of leaves and gets ready to pounce in them.

"One..." She whispers.

"Two..." She pauses.

"Three!" She shouts and watches as Alex's feet leave the boulder before she can even get three out of her mouth.

When Sheila sees Alex down at the bottom, she laughs at him when she sees him smiling up at her. He has leaves collected in his hair, on his brown button-up jacket. Some stuck to his white shoelaces.

"Again!" He shouts, getting out of the pile just for her to make it neat again.

They do this three or four times before Sheila sees someone standing at the trail watching them. She gets down off the boulder and points toward the trail.

"Mom!" Alex shouts at the top of his lungs. She watches as Alex runs just as fast as little legs will carry him.

Sheila watches Kayla gather him into her arms and hold him tightly, twirling him around. She hears the two laughing, and her heart aches.

To have a child, to know what it felt like to have a connection with her own, saddens her knowing that she's not going to have that chance in her life.

Slowly she walks to them when Kayla puts Alex down on his feet and takes his hand. They're waiting for her.

Sheila's surprised that they are since she's only been there a short time taking care of Alex. She can't believe how close they've gotten.

"I am going to make dinner if you want some. I thought that we could have dinner before Alex leaves with his father." Kayla tells her.

Kayla runs a hand through her reddish hair, the sun catching the glint, and her hazel eyes are bright, soft.

Sheila can see that Kayla doesn't like to send Alex away even for the weekend, but adult enough to understand that she has to share.

At twenty-eight, Kayla is smarter than most women are when it comes to a child. Even though she works a lot most times, she takes time for Alex instead of going out and having fun with her friends.

Sheila never sees any of Kayla's friends around, but she doesn't say anything about it. Not sure if she even has any.

"That'd be great." Sheila nods her head as Alex takes her other hand. Then, they continue up the trail toward the house.

Just as they are getting ready to eat dinner, there's a beep outside. Kayla rolls her eyes.

"Daddy!" Alex shouts out, getting up from the dinner table.

"Do you want me to send him out?" Sheila asks, wiping her mouth from the first bite of food that she was able to take.

"No, I think I should do it. I haven't told Ted about the nanny I hired." Kayla sighs, putting down her fork and getting up from the table.

"Alex, wait," Kayla tells him, and he stops in the doorway.

Kayla takes his hand. They head into the living room that comes to the front door where his father is waiting.

Picking up his overnight bag, Kayla opens the door and hands it to his father.

"I didn't think you'd be so early." Kayla looks at the clock on the wall. It's only five in the evening.

"Me neither. I got off work early and thought I'd swing by. I know that I should've called." He runs a hand through his brown hair and stares at her with his brown eyes so intensely that Kayla's not sure if he's lying about how sorry he is.

"That's all right. We had a lot of fun today. Sheila and I went out into the woods, into the field and jumped in some leaves." Alex decides to tell him how his day went right there on the front porch.

"Sheila?" His father asks.

"Ted." Kayla doesn't know how to finish her sentence. She sees the look in his eyes that he's upset and not sure he's going to say.

"Is Sheila a personal friend?" Ted grins at her.

"No, nothing like that," Kayla answers him quickly.

"Really, nothing like the last one where you thought that after a month, I wouldn't find out?" He accuses her.

Kayla's face is getting red. She shuts her mouth and clenches her jaw. The only thing she will refuse to do is argue with Ted in front of Alex.

"Sheila's my nanny," Alex states proudly with a smile on his face as he takes Ted's hand, wanting to go to the car.

"Does Sheila sleep with Mommy?" Ted asks in such a soft voice that you'd have to be listening to hear it.

"No, she doesn't, and I don't think that we should be discussing this in front of Alex. You know that I don't like to be questioned. Even if I were seeing someone, it would be none of your business." Kayla raises her eyebrows at him.

"It would be because Alex is mine too. I want to look out for his best interests." Ted shoots back at her in a friendly tone, but she can see the hate in his brown eyes.

"Come on. I want to go." Alex tugs on Ted's hand, and he finally turns away from the front door.

Alex lets go of his hand and runs back toward the house.

He wraps his arms around his mother's waist and hugs her tightly. Kayla smiles down at him and hugs him back, kissing the top of his head.

"Have fun. I will see you Monday." She tells him, getting down on one knee so that she can talk to him at eye level.

"Let's go, buddy. We're wasting time." Ted calls out to him, opening the back door to the car.

While Ted doesn't show impatience on how much time they spend at the house, she can see it in the way he smiles.

They had been together for three years. Sheila had known everything about him and the vibes he gives off.

Kayla waves when Ted has Alex settled. He puts the window down so Alex can wave, and he gives a honk before they pull out of the driveway.

At least that's one good thing.

When it comes to Alex, Ted can be kind to her. They've come along ways together when it comes to their son. She hopes that it can only get better.

When Kayla shuts the door, she notices that Sheila is standing in the doorway of the living room. She wonders just how much Sheila's heard.

"I'm sorry, sometimes Ted can be..." Kayla lets her voice trail off.

"It's okay. I've had people like that in my life before. Thinking they could control whatever they wanted in my life. I was able to get them out, and I'm better because of it." Sheila nods her head.

"Well, I can't very well just kick Ted out of my life. He's Alex's father. I wanted to sit down and talk with Ted about you being the nanny. Then Alex just came out with it. Ted isn't one for surprises. I meant to tell him earlier in the week. Somehow, it just flew right by." Kayla feels the need to explain a little further.

"There's no need to explain anything to me. All that matters is that Alex is happy, right? I mean, Ted can't make you get rid of me." Sheila gives her a worried look, biting down on her lip.

Kayla doesn't know what she'd do if she weren't taking care of Alex. It was a job. She would have to worry about how she was going to get another one, but that wasn't all. She was beginning to love Alex. She could see that Alex was getting closer to her.

Sheila didn't want to lose that bond.

"There's no way that he would tell me that I couldn't find someone for Alex. He knows that I have to work. He gave me the house. There's no way that he'd want to see me fail. If I'm failing, that means

Alex will be too. Neither of us wants that." Kayla clears her throat.

To know that Sheila had heard everything that came out of Ted's mouth makes her blush. It makes her hotter than the weather outside.

"I'm going to take a dip in the pool. Would you like to join me?" Kayla asks.

"That would be wonderful. I don't know how many days it's going to be like this." Sheila laughs.

Kayla goes upstairs to her room to get changed, closing the door behind her while Sheila goes to her room down the hall and feels even happier knowing that Kayla didn't just lock herself into her home office like she does when she's home working.

# Chapter Two

By the time they get out to the pool, the sun is already setting, but it's still humid as Sheila makes a face running a hand through her hair, not liking how it feels.

"I think this is what they call Indian summer. I'm so glad that we have a pool. I can't imagine trying to go to the gym and relaxing." Kayla giggles a little.

Sheila can't seem to keep her eyes off Kayla in her white bikini that she's wearing the way it fits her perfectly.

Kayla can see the way that Sheila's looking at her from the corner of her eye and wonders if Ted might be right.

She closes her eyes and thinks about what it might be like with Sheila. She's a little younger than she is. She remembers the last time that Ted had found her with another woman.

"What did Ted mean about me being in your bed?" Sheila asks, breaking Kayla out of her thoughts before she could begin to enjoy them.

"I'm sorry that you had to hear that. I didn't think you did." Kayla shakes her head, opening her eyes and noticing how close Sheila is to her. She bites down on her lip.

Kayla sees the pink two-piece that Sheila's wearing, she notices how tight it is on her, wondering if that's the only suit that she had packed with her.

"It's not a big deal." Sheila shrugs her shoulders and takes her eyes away from Kayla's to look at the sunset.

The sun is bright orange. She knows that it's going to be hotter tomorrow. Indian summer has definitely come.

"When Ted and I first split up, I was seeing this woman. I thought it might be different. I guess after a few months, I decided to make it official. I told Ted about it since he should know because he is Alex's father. He's right about that. Well, when I came out with it, the woman didn't want to be here anymore. She didn't want anyone knowing, I suppose. I thought we were on the same page. Apparently, we weren't." Kayla shrugs one of her shoulders, but Sheila can see the hurt there.

"I'm sorry that you went through all that trouble." She whispers to her.

"It's all right. I mean, Alex didn't know. So, it couldn't hurt him. He just knew her as a babysitter on the weekends when he was home. He didn't know how close we were. When it comes to Alex, I don't want him hurt in any way. She would come over at night when Alex was sleeping, sometimes he would see her in the hall, but he's too young to understand it all even now." Kayla explained.

"You don't have to explain anything to me. I see how you are with Alex. How much you love him. You work too much. I think, at the same time, I know why you're doing it." Sheila smiles at her, giving her the courage to smile herself.

"What about you? Do you have a family? Someone you love. I know that we haven't taken the time to get to know each other. I'm afraid that's my fault." Kayla blushes.

She knows that Sheila's right. That she works way too damn much, but she can't get out of the mode when her anxiety kicks in and tells her that she has to work even harder than the day before to make ends meet.

"I don't have anyone that I'm interested in. I mean, sometimes I go out on dates, but it's rare. I guess I haven't found the right person yet." Sheila swims a little further away from Kayla after the words are out of her mouth.

"Well, maybe I can hook you up with someone. Who knows, they might be the one. Ted has a few handsome business partners. Not for me, but they are good-looking." Kayla swims after her.

"I don't think that they would be my type, either." Sheila laughs, swimming toward the deep end, spinning around and leaning her back against the wall, bringing her arms up and over so that she can lift her legs and let them float.

"What do you mean by that?" Kayla asks, treading water before she touches Sheila's feet.

"Why did you and Ted break up?" Sheila asks, wanting to change the subject, not wanting to tell Kayla everything all at once.

"It was my fault," Kayla feels her face growing hot. She doesn't want to talk about it. She doesn't want to think back to when she was a horrible person.

"Don't be so hard on yourself." Sheila shakes her head.

There's no way that Kayla could be the bad guy, as sweet as she was. As lovely as she was, Sheila just can't picture it.

"He came home from work early one day. I have to admit that I was entertaining someone upstairs while Alex was away for the day with my mother. It was a great time. I have to admit that. However, when he came into the house and walked up the stairs. When he stood in the doorway, I knew that it was over between us." She whispers.

"Really?" Sheila's eyes grow big, focusing on the words that are coming out of Kayla's mouth.

"Really. Ted still can't get over the fact to this day." Kayla shakes her head.

Ted still talks about it, even though it happened a long time ago. He also thought she wouldn't change what had happened. Sometimes she wishes that she wouldn't see the hurt in his eyes when he picks up Alex.

She can tell when Ted's having a good day or a bad day just by the look in his eyes. He tries to cover it up, but she knows him.

"He can't get over the fact that you were with another man?" Sheila asks her.

"No, he can't get over the fact that I was with another woman. I didn't cheat on him with a man. I held this secret for so long that I was into women more than men. There were a few times that I wanted to tell him. I wanted to state it. However, there was never the right time." Kayla shakes her head back and forth, her reddish hair swaying with her head.

There's a moment of silence. Sheila stares up at the sky that's getting darker by the second. She likes hearing the birds in the trees overhead talking to each other.

"Okay, now why don't you want a man in your life?" Kayla asks.

She knows that it's only fair that Sheila tells her something personal about herself since she had done the same thing.

"I don't prefer men." Sheila looks at her, raises her eyebrows, and feels a grin come to her face when she sees a small smirk on Kayla's face.

"That's why it didn't bother you when you heard what Ted said. If it were anyone else, they would've defended themselves." Kayla laughs a little.

"Right. Not to mention, I don't feel the need to defend myself. I don't care what anyone thinks of me. I don't entertain people who think that they can get me upset." Sheila pushes away from the wall to swim back to the shallow end of the pool.

Her heart is racing. She can't believe that she just told her boss that she was into women! How could she let that out?

Then again, Kayla didn't look at Sheila differently. Sheila didn't look at her like she was an alien, like most of her family had when she had come out about who she was.

Their dreams were shot down by the way she feels. Something that she still hasn't gotten over herself, but she doesn't want to think about that now.

She's been happy. She wants to be more content without having to think about the ones that bring her down.

"I think that you will find the right woman one of these days," Kayla tells her when she touches the railing of the shallow water.

"Yeah, I'm getting too old now. Too old for babies like my mother wants, too old for wanting to have a man like my mother wants. Too old to find happiness." She shakes her head.

"Like your mother wants?" Kayla asks.

"No, like I want." Sheila smiles at her.

They stare at each other for a moment. Kayla licks her lips. She knows what she wants to do, but she doesn't want to take advantage of Sheila in a weak moment.

"You don't know how beautiful you are," Kayla tells her and pushes off the railing to swim to the middle of the pool. She leaves Sheila to her thoughts about what Kayla had just said.

Sheila giggles a little, Then, she bites down on her lip and shakes her head.

Maybe Kayla was just saying it to make her feel better. She didn't know, but she was feeling a little happier since she'd been talking with Kayla.

"What do you do for fun?" Sheila asks when she pulls herself out of the pool and grabs a towel that's on the patio chair.

"I like to go out dancing sometimes. You want to go out dancing tomorrow night?" Kayla asks her.

Dancing was one of the things Sheila feels too old to do.

"Come on, let your wild side hang out. You know you want to." Kayla laughs at her, pulling herself up from the pool herself.

"Sure. I mean, I haven't done anything really wild. I don't have anything to wear out," Sheila confesses to her.

"We're about the same height and same size. You can try something on. I know just the outfit that I want you to wear. I bet you'd look good in it." Kayla thinks about it for a second.

"Yeah?" Sheila raises her eyebrows.

"Yeah, let's go play dress up." Kayla giggles, taking her by the hand and leading her into the house without thinking about it.

Kayla is happy to see the smile on Sheila's face. They had gone from important conversation to playing around in just a matter of seconds.

Kayla loved it that way. She liked it when she could be serious with someone one second and then fun-loving the next.

Sheila went into Kayla's room for the first time. She immediately sees the king-sized bed, along with her white blankets. Everything in Sheila's bedroom

is white—the rug, the dressers, and the closet doors. Kayla made her way to the closet. Then she opened the doors wide, pushing them against the wall.

Kayla pulls out an outfit that's on a hanger. Sheila looks at it and shakes her head, laughing at her.

"Come on, be daring. Try it on." Kayla pushes it toward her.

Kayla smiles when Sheila takes it.

Sheila turns and walks out of the room with it. Going across the hall to the bathroom, Sheila closes the door and leans against it.

Looking at the outfit, she sees how the leather stretches. She's sure that it's going to fit. Sheila isn't sure how she's going to look in it.

"Here's to new changes." She giggles as she slowly gets out of the bikini and grabs a towel to dry off.

She makes sure that she is completely dry before putting on the outfit. She wants to make sure that it fits her properly.

However, just looking at the outfit, she can see that there's nothing proper about it.

# Chapter Three

Sheila tries on the skin-tight dress. She looks at herself in the mirror. Her blonde hair is damp from the pool water. She looks at her blue eyes that are already tired.

"What are you doing?" She laughs at herself in the mirror.

"Sheila, come on, you're taking forever," Kayla calls out to her.

"I don't think I'm ready to come out," she calls back to her.

"You are if you have that dress on!" Kayla laughs at her.

Sheila opens the door. She sees Kayla standing in the doorway of her bedroom with her dress on.

It's red, the straps are thin, and the bottom of the dress barely covers her hips. She can see the matching red panties that she has on underneath.

"You go out dancing in that?" Sheila's eyes grow wide.

"Sometimes, I do. Do you think it's too revealing?" Kayla bites down on her lip and sizes up Sheila's body in the dress.

Sheila's breasts are pushed together. Her hair looks as if she's just gotten out of the shower. And, her long legs make her look younger than she is.

"I think that you should wear that dress tomorrow night." Kayla nods her head in approval.

"I feel silly in it." Sheila yanks down the sides of her dress, trying to make it a little longer.

"Either that or you can find another dress that looks more like mine. It's easier to dance in, something that's not, leather." Kayla turns around. Sheila can't help but notice the way her hips whip back and forth, making the back of the dress come up just a little.

"I wouldn't wear that tomorrow night unless you want the men to think that you're willing to go home with them." Sheila points out to her, walking into the room.

"We can both wear matching, black dresses," Kayla calls to her from the closet, taking out two more dresses.

Shelia likes the fabric. When Kayla hands it to her, she's able to bring the dress down just a little so that it won't look too short on her.

"Yes, I'd love to wear matching dresses." Sheila nods her head in approval at the dress that Kayla has handed to her.

"Good, it's not often that I go out. I don't want you to think that I go out every weekend. I just get the urge to let loose sometimes." She points out to her.

"You should have that time for you. You work too much." Sheila shakes her head.

"I have a lot of responsibilities on my shoulders. I can't just sit still. I can't just work an eight- hour shift and call it good. You know that Alex is growing like a weed. Soon he's going to be above my hip." She laughs a little.

Sheila can hear it in her voice that she misses Alex. That she wishes that he was here with them. But, at the same time, she also sees the woman that should be going out and having a good time. She's single. There's no reason why Sheila can't.

"You really want me to go with you?" Sheila bites down on her lip.

"I wouldn't have asked you if I didn't want you going." Kayla points a finger at her.

Sheila turns back around to head to the bathroom. Kayla lets her eyes roam up and down the back of her dress.

She silently wishes that Sheila would have more confidence in her body. The dress looks hot on her. She looks a lot younger than her age.

Kayla closes her bedroom door and gets undressed. She gets into her white, fluffy, robe and ties it tightly around her.

Getting on the bed, she lies down and turns the television on. Wanting to watch a movie, but there's nothing good on when she flips through the channels.

There's a knock on her bedroom door. She smiles, shaking her head.

"You can come in. You don't have to knock." Kayla tells her.

"I don't like just walking into anyone's room, that's not who I am," Sheila tells her.

"That's good to know. Around here, there's not much privacy. I feel weird with you knocking on my door." Kayla laughs a little.

"What room is that down the hallway?" Sheila asks.

"My old exercising room before I had a home gym installed. Nothing really." Kayla shrugs her shoulders.

Sheila gets ready to walk out of the room when Kayla calls her name. She looks back over her shoulder.

"You don't always have to stay in your room if you don't want to. I notice that when you put Alex to bed, that's where you go." Kayla tells her.

"I didn't know you noticed with that office door of yours only slightly ajar." Sheila smiles at her.

"I notice a lot more than you think," Kayla assures her.

"What do you want to do then? It's Friday night. It's not even ten at night, and we are both inside. It looks like you're getting ready for bed yourself." Sheila points out to her, raising her eyebrows and giving a small smirk.

"I don't know what do you normally do?" Kayla askes, sitting up on the bed and making room for Sheila to sit down.

Sheila sits on the edge of the bed and leaves the door open to the bedroom. Not sure exactly what she wants to do.

"What I would normally do is have a glass of wine and some pretzels." She shakes her head, feeling ashamed of it.

"The way I saw you with Alex today. I watched you for a good couple of minutes. Each time he jumped into the leaves, Alex was on top of the world. I know that he likes you. I like you too. It might seem strange huh?" Kayla asks.

"What's strange?" Sheila asks.

She smiles at the memory that she shared with Alex. Sheila didn't realize Kayla was sharing the same memory as her.

"The way we get attached to people so easily. At one time, you were a stranger to us. And now, it's almost like we've known you forever." Kayla tells her.

Her voice is confident, not the least bit of hesitation in her voice.

"I don't think that it's strange at all. I think that in a world that's so tough on us, we should consider the ones who come into our lives and leaving a mark a rare jewel. That's how we should treat them. If everyone treated each other with respect, I don't think that we'd have so many issues in the world." Sheila tells her.

It's incredible how easy it is to talk to Kayla. Especially talking with someone who is slightly younger and who grasps how Sheila feels inside.

It's in that silence that Kayla kisses her softly. She doesn't even think about it. Kayla just does it. It feels good that she can be so courageous.

Sheila feels her soft lips against Kayla's. She likes the way it feels. Sheila kisses her back just as slowly. Kayla gasps when Sheila slips her tongue into her mouth.

"I'm sorry. I shouldn't have done that." Sheila pulls her mouth away from hers.

"No, it's all right. I wanted you to. It's been so long, too long," Kayla murmurs, licking her lips. She remembers the moment Sheila's tongue touched hers.

She wonders how far it would've gone if she hadn't made a noise and just let Sheila do her thing.

"I don't think that it would be wise to do that with my boss. I mean, first it starts with a kiss and then before you know it there are feelings involved and if something was to happen that neither one of us wanted." Sheila continues to ramble on. That's when Kayla laughs at her and kisses her again. This time she kisses Sheila harder as she brings a hand to the back of Sheila's head.

She thrusts her tongue into Sheila's mouth. Sheila moans for her, reaching out and touching the sides of Kayla's face, showing her that her words don't match her actions.

Kayla grabs a handful of Sheila's hair and brings Sheila even closer. She hurts Sheila's lips, but it feels so good.

The only reason why Sheila pulls away this time is so that she can catch her breath. Instead of staying on the bed, Sheila walks out of the room. She goes to the bathroom, closing the door behind her.

She leans against the bathroom counter for a few seconds, her legs shaking, her heart racing. She doesn't exactly know what she's doing.

She looks at herself in the mirror and shakes her head.

"You know that this is dangerous." She whispers to her reflection. She can't allow herself to fall for her boss.

When Sheila collects herself, she sees that Kayla's door is still open. Sheila goes down the hall to her room and closes the door.

If Sheila were to go back in there tonight, she knows what would happen. Sheila knows that she would get attached and do something she would think about later. Maybe not regret but wonder how she could've done things differently.

Sheila licks her lips, feeling Kayla's lips against hers still. She half hopes that Kayla will come to her, half hopes that she leaves it alone for tonight.

Sheila tosses and turns throughout the night, not hearing the door open. Sheila does hear Kayla leave the bedroom even to go to the bathroom.

Early in the morning, when the sun starts coming out, Sheila is up and looking out her window. She can see the pool down below. She knows that if she were to jump out the window, she would land in the deep end.

"It's fun jumping into the pool from there. I've tried it a time or two." She hears her bedroom door open, hears Kayla's voice.

"Good morning." Sheila turns and smiles at her, hoping that last night was behind them.

"Good morning. How did you sleep?" Kayla asks.

"Like shit." She laughs.

"Me too. Let's go downstairs and make some coffee." She tells me, turning and walking out of the room, leaving the door open.

Kayla hadn't slept a wink last night, thinking about the way Sheila had kissed her so furiously. The need, the want that was inside of her, letting it out little by little.

She didn't think that Sheila would walk out of the room. Kayla didn't think that Sheila would just go to her room and sleep.

Kayla was hoping for something more.

That's when she realized that maybe Sheila just wasn't ready. Perhaps she wasn't used to a younger woman hitting on her.

Kayla knows that she's ready to start another chapter of her life. She's ready to show the world that she wants to be with someone intimately.

The nights are lonely without someone. Kayla knows that she can handle the lonely nights that it has nothing to do with wanting to use Shelia because she'd been alone too long.

By the time that Kayla comes downstairs, the coffee is ready. Kayla takes out two cups. Sheila makes her own, then Kayla does.

"Are we still on for tonight?" Kayla asks her.

"I wouldn't miss it for the world. Do you know how long it's been since I've been out to a club?" Sheila asks, taking her first sip without even blowing on it first.

"A long time, I'm guessing. The way you looked at those dresses, it seems that your style might be out of date." Kayla teases her.

Sheila laughs, she doesn't feel the tension between them thinking that Kayla was going to hold it against her for running away last night.

# Chapter Four

Sheila and Kayla work out together. They swim together. They talk more about what they want to do in the future. Kayla can see that Sheila has her own goals that have nothing to do with the world, even though Sheila believes that her future is nothing but a pipe dream.

Knowing that Shelia wants to travel the world, is something that makes Kayla sad. Now that they can talk without interruption, she likes Shelia even more than she had when she first started watching Alex.

"I think that if you went around the world traveling that Alex and I would both miss you." Kayla finds the nerve to speak up.

"I don't even know how I would get the money to go traveling." Sheila laughs a little.

"I would give you an advance if that was something that you were serious about." Kayla can't believe just what she has said.

Willing to help Sheila leave her life, something that she didn't even want.

"No, I wouldn't do something like that to you. You gave me this job to watch Alex. I would never abandon you like that. Not even if…" Sheila doesn't want to say the next words that are about to come from her mouth.

"Not even if what?" Kayla pushes her.

"Not even if we were to get intimate with each other, and things didn't work out. That's all I was going to say." She clears her throat.

Kayla doesn't know what to say about it. That's when the tension starts to brew. She doesn't like the fact that Sheila is making it sound like such a big deal.

She's the one who had walked out of her room and didn't come back in. Sheila is the one who ran away from the situation at hand.

Kayla gets up before she can say anything that would be too hurtful and goes into the house, going to her room and slamming the bedroom door.

Sheila knows that the words that were said were something that she should've never said.

Then again, Kayla never should've pushed her to get the words out.

Sheila finds herself getting up from the patio chair and going into the house. She goes upstairs quietly. She sees that Kayla's bedroom door is closed.

Sheila thinks about going into her room. However, it isn't something that she should do. Sheila can't simply turn away from the problem at hand. She wants to fix it before they go to the club, and before Alex comes home on Monday.

Without knocking, Sheila opens the door and sees that Kayla is pacing back and forth with her hands behind her back.

"I don't understand what the matter is with you," Sheila whispers, not wanting to step over the line of making her more upset than she already is.

"Why don't you like me?" Kayla comes out with it, making Sheila take a step back.

"What are you talking about?" Sheila asks her, confused.

"Is it because I'm too young? Is it because I have a child? What is it? Because I'm your boss?" Kayla gets the words out of her mouth as fast as she can before she loses her damn nerve.

"I do like you," Sheila tells her, shaking her head.

"Yeah? If you liked me so much, then why did you leave my room last night? Why did you walk out of here like it was hell?" Kayla narrows her eyes, her face getting red.

"You think it's because I don't like you?" Sheila asks her, snorting a little and shaking her head back and forth as she puts her hands on her hips.

"What else can it be?" Kayla points a finger at her, not wanting to hear any lies.

"I like you a lot. That kiss was amazing. Both of them were. You just don't understand. I don't want to jump into something and then have it not work out. I can't have that happen to me, not in my own life." Sheila mutters.

"You don't take risks. You don't like the fact that something so good could be so scary. You don't like to get out of control." Kayla tells her accusingly.

"So, what if that's what the issue is?" Sheila asks her.

"You can't live your life like that. You're never going to be happy if you don't go with the flow of things. To find out if something is truly there. I believe that there's something between us already. The connection that we have, the bond that's growing between us. It's not just about Alex. If that were the case, I would've made plans last night without even involving you." Kayla mutters, shaking her head.

Sheila doesn't know what else to say. She doesn't know what to do. The one thing that she doesn't do is walk out of the room.

With each step that she takes closer and closer to Kayla, she feels the emotions running through her, the want from last night.

It does scare her, Kayla's right about that. But she's right about a lot of things.

Sheila brings her mouth to Kayla's and kisses her softly. Sheila licks Kayla's lips with the tip of her tongue. Her tongue runs around Kayla's lips and makes them so wet.

Kayla moans as she brings her hands around to hold Sheila's ass cheeks in the palms of her hand. How round they are, she squeezes them gently and caresses them. Kayla doesn't want to scare her away this time.

"I want you. Don't think for a second that I don't," Sheila whisper against Kayla's mouth.

"Show me that you want me, and I might believe you." Kayla challenges her and feels Sheila's hands slide up her back. She feels Sheila's hands untying the string that holds her bikini top up. She feels it falling away from her.

Sheila strips her of her bikini bottom so that she's completely naked in front of her. She takes a step back and sees the beautiful tanned body in front of her.

Sheila's breasts are perky. Her nipples are getting harder as Kayla stands in front of her, not moving.

Sheila lowers her eyes to her mound between her legs and sees how nicely shaved it is. It looks so good just the way it looks at the moment.

"Sheila," Kayla whispers to her, running her hand through her hair and watching Sheila's eyes move up and down with them.

Sheila gets out of her bathing suit and goes to the edge of the bed. She sits down at the end of the bed and stares at her.

Without a word, Kayla goes to her, sitting down beside her and just staring into her eyes.

"Kayla," Sheila whispers so softly, her voice is shaking. When Sheila lays down on the bed, Kayla doing the same thing.

Kayla runs a hand up and down the side of Sheila's body. Kayla sees the goose pimples that show up on her skin.

"Let's get this out of the way before we hit the dance floor tonight," Kayla whispers to her, pressing her mouth against Sheila's slowly getting on top of her and running her hand through Sheila's hair.

Sheila feels her heart thumping hard against her chest. She feels their nubs getting harder together. Sheila opens her legs a little wider so that Kayla can dip down between them with her smoothness against hers.

"Yes, just like that. I love how you feel against me." Kayla whimpers against her mouth.

Sheila spreads her legs just a little wider for her, wider and wider each time that Kayla nods her head at her.

Sheila feels Kayla grinding against her, feeling her lips spreading slowly. She moans herself when she feels Kayla's clit pressing against hers, sliding up and down hers.

"This is something that could've happened last night. Maybe then we would've gotten some sleep." Kayla thrusts her tongue into Sheila's mouth.

"Kayla, God, Kayla." Sheila gasps against her mouth and tugs on her hair.

Kayla closes her eyes, feeling their tongues touching each other, wanting each other, their bodies coming alive.

It doesn't take long for the girls to cum for each other, soaking each other and smelling the sweetness between them.

"Damn. Oh, damn!" Kayla cries out as she feels the wetness between them. She doesn't want to stop as she slides her body up and down Sheila's faster and faster, the panting that she feels against her ear that's coming from Sheila's mouth now.

Sheila can feel her heart racing against Kayla's as if they're one now when Kayla lays there on top of her trying to catch her breath, trying to compose herself.

"Now, that was amazing. That was showing me that you truly want me." Kayla whispers against her ear, licking at her earlobe with the tip of her tongue.

"I have a hard time showing my emotions. I don't want it to be like this one day, and then we ignore each other the next. You have no idea how many times that's happened to me. Something doesn't work out or go as planned. We start to hate each other." Sheila whispers.

"No, that's not how it's going to be between the two of us. I'm not going to let it the more you get to know me, the more you'll see for yourself. Let me show you that I'm not like the rest Sheila. Let me show you that I want you." Kayla whispers, pressing her mouth against Sheila's ear and hoping that it will sink in.

Sheila nods her head. Kayla knows that not everyone is the same. Kayla has to give Sheila a chance. If she were to push every female away, Kayla knows that she will never find the true happiness that she wants.

She will be alone, and the what-ifs would be going through her head when she could've silenced them.

"Yeah? Do you want to try this with me?" Kayla pulls away from her and when Sheila can see her face, she sees that there's a smile there.

"I want to try this with you. I want to see where it's going to go." Sheila tells her softly.

Kayla hugs her tightly and feels Shelia's arms come around her, holding her just as tightly. Kayla feels the loneliness slowly disappearing.

"We're destined to be together," Kayla assures her, kissing her one more time on the mouth before she gets up and leaves the bedroom without getting dressed.

A few minutes later, Sheila laughs, hearing the shower turning on in the bathroom as she lays there and stares up at the ceiling with the smile spreading wider across her face.

"I don't know what I'm getting myself into, but I know that I like it," Sheila whispers to herself and sits up on the bed.

Sheila tries not to think about how the future is going to go for them. She doesn't want to stress herself out thinking that she has to change who she is.

Kayla likes her for her. That's all she has to remind herself of.

When Kayla gets out of the shower, Sheila gets into the shower and doesn't realize how late it's getting until Kayla puts the dress that she's going to wear to the club on the counter.

"Are you sure you want to go out tonight?" Sheila asks, shutting the shower off and rubbing her body down with a towel.

"Yes! I think that it's going to be amazing for both of us." Kayla tells her, confident that the night is only going to get better for them.

Sheila puts the dress on she chose. Sheila likes the way it fits her body. She also likes the way her body moves with it when she does a side-step, pretending that she's on the dance floor.

## Chapter Five

Sheila and Kayla make their way out onto the dance floor.  Sheila loves the confidence that Kayla has when she takes her hand and brings her out into the middle of the floor, dancing to a fast song. She is a little embarrassed when Kayla begins to grind against her. Kayla rubs her hips against Sheila's, then finds her rhythm. Kayla likes the way she dances and the way their bodies mash against each other.

They dance off and on throughout the night. They drink water, knowing that one of them is going to have to drive.

Sheila looks around and sees that the men and the women are looking at Kayla. They are noticing her more and more.

She feels a pang of jealousy inside of her.

"Don't you worry about who wants me. As long as I want you, that's all you need to know." Kayla whispers against Sheila's ear, making Sheila's face turn red.

Sheila wasn't sure that Kayla was paying attention to the way the men and women were looking at her, the expression on her face.

Sheila nods her head as Kayla pulls her back out on the dance floor. Some men are trying to get in between them. However, Kayla isn't going to let that happen. She notices how Kayla dances around them just to get back to her.

"Are you almost ready to leave?" Kayla whispers in Sheila's ear as she pulls her closer, feeling their breasts pressing against each other.

Kayla slides her body up and down Sheila's and hears her moan against her ear as she nods her head.

"Good, I think that I've had enough dancing for one night." Kayla giggles and pulls away from her and takes her by her hand tightly.

Sheila is glad that Kayla is holding on so tightly. The crowd is getting bigger and bigger. Sheila knows that she'd be lost in the crowd of people if Kayla wasn't watching out for her.

"God, it feels so good out here!" Kayla shouts out into the quiet night.

Sheila laughs at her, but she silently admits the fresh air after being in the club is welcoming. It's almost ten o'clock at night. She never realized how fast time could go.

Getting into the car, Kayla starts it. Sheila gets her seatbelt on.

"Do all the men and women look at you like that when you go out?" Sheila asks her.

"Yes, that's why I don't go out alone. Ted never liked going out with me. There would always be an agreement if I went out with my friends. That's why I didn't go out often. When I became single, I told myself that I would never allow someone to make me feel bad for having a good time." She shrugs her shoulders.

They leave the parking lot, but they don't head back for Kayla's house. Sheila doesn't know where they're going until she smells the ocean breeze when she rolls down the window.

"I like to escape from reality a lot. One minute I could be at the club and the next here at the ocean where it's nice and quiet." Kayla doesn't take her eyes off the road until she's completely parked.

Shutting off the car and leaving the headlights on, she grins at Sheila and gets out of the vehicle. Sheila laughs at her when she watches her run down to the water. Sheila watches Kayla kick up the sand under her bare feet.

"Hey! Get out here!" Kayla shouts to her. Sheila gets out of the car the second she hears her voice.

She goes running down to the sand, and they run into the ocean together.

"This is crazy, do you know that?" Sheila hollers out to Kayla above the noise of the surf.

"It's what I like to do. I like to have a lot of fun. I work a lot, but when I let loose, I let loose." Kayla giggles, going waist-deep into the ocean before running back out.

Kayla feels the coolness on her skin. Her dress sticks to her. She knows she's going to keep the memory for the rest of her life.

"We didn't even bring extra clothes," Sheila tells her, knowing that they're going to get the seats wet in the car.

"You always live by the rules. For once, just let it all go. Let yourself go." Kayla throws her head back and laughs as they race to the car.

Sheila can't remember the last time she had so much fun with anyone. She'd never met anyone like Kayla. Seeing her when she doesn't have to worry about anything excites her. It makes Sheila even happier knowing that Kayla wants to be with her.

Kayla turns the heat on before she even bothers leaving the ocean. They're both shivering, teeth chattering.

"This was a great night. I don't care. It's one of the books." Sheila giggles, feeling her teeth clank against each other.

"Same, I haven't done anything like this in a very long time. Ted was just too boring. He didn't like to take risks. He always lived by the rules. The other one didn't want to be seen in public with me." Kayla shakes off the horrible feeling of that time.

"I think that anyone would be lucky to have you by their side," Sheila tells her, taking her hand and holding it tightly.

"Me too," Kayla tells her. Then, they go into another fit of giggles as if they're high school kids. Sheila laughs until her sides and lungs ache.

"Are you ready to go back to the house?" Kayla asks when the car is nice and heated.

"Yes. I am ready to call it a night." Sheila nods her head, and Kayla pulls out of the parking lot. She lets the ocean alone, once again.

By the time they get back to the house, it's almost one in the morning. They climb the stairs and get into something dryer.

"Where are you going?" Kayla asks as she watches Sheila leave the bathroom and head down the hall.

"I thought that you might want some space. Some time for yourself." Sheila shrugs her shoulders.

"If I wanted space, I would tell you. Unless you don't want to share my bed tonight." Kayla grins at her.

Sheila loves how hazel her eyes are. The twinkle in her eyes shows Sheila that Kayla doesn't want to call it a night. She doesn't want the night to end at all.

She goes into the bedroom and lays on the other side of the bed. Pulling the blanket back and feeling her body relax.

"Tonight was nice. Thanks for going out with me. I honestly didn't think that you would, you surprised me." Kayla nods her head, looking over at her.

"You thought I was going to cancel on you?" Sheila asks, a little offended by the idea.

"Well, after today, I didn't think that you would have the energy to go." Kayla winks at her. Sheila feels her heart skip a beat.

These are the moments she wants to hold closer. If she were in her room, she would have been thinking about how great the day had been.

"Are you going to go back to the working momma when Alex comes home? I mean hiding yourself behind the doors and not coming out even for dinner?" Sheila asks her.

"I don't know. I mean, I like the fun that we're having right now. I know that I have to balance my work. I can't just be ghost the whole time now that you're here. You don't know how hard it was before you showed up. The only time I was able to work was when Alex was in bed. Even then, that was a struggle, as you know for yourself." Kayla points out to her.

Sheila nods her head, looking into Kayla's eyes. She can see that far off look on her face. She knows that she's going to contemplate what's going to happen.

"I do know that I'm going to try my best to start with simple things like joining you guys at dinner. Taking small breaks here and there so that Alex doesn't feel ignored so that you don't feel ignored. There are two people that I need to share my time with now." Kayla giggles. Sheila can hear the emotion in her laughter.

"It's not that hard. I can help you with that. We'll make a timesheet of when you can take breaks. It'll show how long you're allowed to break. When you're done for the night, even if you don't finish, there's always another day for it. I used to plan days out, remember?" Sheila asks her.

"That's right. The daycare center. You must miss it there a lot," Kayla tells her, feeling sad for Sheila.

"Not really. I mean, it's not like I got fired. Everyone lost their jobs because the owner wasn't keeping up with it. That wasn't our fault. Besides, if I had never left the center, I wouldn't know you or Alex, right?" Sheila shrugs her shoulders.

"We would've met up one way or another. If it's meant to be, there's always a way." Kayla raises one eyebrow at her.

Sheila sees that Kayla believes in magic when it comes to love. No matter how many times she's let down, she still believes that there's magic.

"I think you're right. We might've met up at the grocery store, the ocean. Definitely not the club. You wouldn't catch me out at the club unless invited." Sheila laughs at the thought of doing it on her own.

"Yeah, I see that. You need to come out of your shell too. If you help me learn how to take a little time off work, then I'm going to show you how young you really are." Kayla promises her.

"I can't wait until Alex comes back home. I have to say that I miss chasing him around the house." Sheila stares off at the television screen that's not even on.

"I have to say that it's been a little dull without him around. He would have laughed if he saw me tonight." Kayla giggles a little.

"I would say that he would look at you as if he didn't know who you are." Sheila agrees with her, feeling even better that they can talk about Alex almost on the same level.

Kayla takes Sheila's hand in hers. Kayla lets her smile fade just a little.

"What's the matter?" Sheila asks, spotting trouble a mile away.

"I just don't want this good feeling to end. I want to be able to come up to you and hug you even when Alex is here. I want to be able to kiss you even if it's just for a second whether Alex is in the room or not." Kayla confesses to her.

"Nothing is going to stop you from doing that." Sheila insists.

"Yeah? If we venture into this, I don't want Alex to get hurt either. I know that I want you. I want to get to know more about you. I don't think that Ted should know about this just yet. I mean, after the last time." She sighs and shakes her head.

        "He doesn't have to know anything. Neither does Alex if you don't want him to. It's just that the three of us would be spending more time together. Then we would become closer. To tell you the truth, I think that Alex needs that. I'm not telling you what to do, but I do know that he was happy when the three of us were walking back up the trail together before we had dinner." Sheila points out to her, kissing the back of Kayla's hand to show her that everything is going to just fine if she lets it be.

# Chapter Six

Kayla looks over at Sheila, hearing the words from her mouth, feeling the romance already starting. The butterflies that she has, she can't stop smiling at her.

She also knows that it's not fair to keep Sheila from anyone. Kayla just doesn't want anyone knowing until she knows it's a sure thing.

"You know why I'm doing this right?" Kayla asks softly.

"You don't want to get burned again. You don't want your family burned again," Sheila tells her with confidence.

She understands the pain and stress that Kayla had once gone through. Sheila didn't want Kayla to worry about repeating it.

"Right. With you wanting to travel," Kayla remembers their talk from earlier.

"It doesn't mean that I'm going to do that right off. I don't even have anything mapped out, no clothes for the weather of other states. I wouldn't worry about that." Sheila tells her softly, shaking her head back and forth.

That was one thing that she wished she hadn't told Kayla about. Seeing how young she was, seeing that she would think that it was a plan that she was going to follow in a snap of a finger.

"I'm not going to sit there and leave you and Alex to fend for yourselves. I don't even know if I'm going to do it. It's a dream. That's all it is." Sheila closes her eyes in hopes that the conversation will be dropped.

Kayla pulls her hand away and gets comfortable under the sheet, putting her head on Sheila's stomach and smiling. Thinking about the night's events and how crazy they had been.

It was fun.

She didn't have fun like that anymore. Not since she had been with Ted, not since she had become a mother. It felt good to have the freedom.

"I want this to work, Kayla. You know that, right?" Sheila asks, running a hand through Kayla's hair.

"I know that." She nods her head and thinks about the future, what it might hold for them.

"I found out tonight that you had a wild side. You brought mine out, making me feel younger than what I am." Sheila giggles.

"That's because you are younger than your age. You don't act old. I don't think that you're old. If you hadn't told me your age during the interview, I would've thought that you were the same age as me." Kayla points out to her, lifting her head just a little.

"How many people were ahead of me for the job?" Sheila asks her.

"Three, they were nothing like you. Quite ditzy about the job if you ask me. I need someone who can have fun with Alex. I also know that there's a line that has to drawn when it comes to what they do and his safety." Kayla explains to her.

"That's true. I know how to be safe and fun. When to be serious and when to be free-spirited, I guess." Sheila feels a smile come to her face.

"Alex enjoys his time with you. I can see it on his face when I look out the window. And, when I see the two of you playing in his room as I pass by. He does like you. I don't think that he's liked anyone as much as he does you." Kayla feels a warm smile come to her face.

It was all about Alex in the beginning. She had hoped that Sheila would work out for the sake of Alex. It was nice to have someone else around the house.

"I'm sorry that Ted was hurtful to you when he picked up Alex. I know when to mind my business, but does he do that often to you?" Sheila asks.

"What do you mean?" Kayla lifts her head just enough to look into Sheila's eyes.

"I mean the way he tries to tell you to do things. The snide comments that he made about having another woman in your bed." Sheila grunts, shaking her head.

"He brings it up a lot when it's just the two of us. Alex is either getting his things ready, or he's already in the car. I choose to ignore it most of the time. He doesn't understand why I would be with a woman, I guess. It hurts worse that he found out I was with a female instead of a male." Kayla shrugs her shoulders.

They fall asleep with Kayla laying her head back down on Sheila's stomach, with Sheila running a hand through her hair.

Sheila drifts off with a smile on her face in hopes that things continue to get better between her and Kayla.

The last thing she wants to do is hurt Kayla and Alex. Going with the flow seems like a good idea. Yet, she can't help but want to jump right into the family thing with the two of them.


The alarm goes off early in the morning. Sheila groans at the feel of the sun coming through the window onto her face.

"Let's go. We don't have time to waste today. We have to get the house in order. We have to make sure that Alex has clothes for the week. I have to get laundry done." Kayla laughs when Sheila squints her eyes.

"Are you always like this?" Sheila groans, bringing a pillow to her face to block out the sun.

"No, I'm happier." She giggles and tries to tug the pillow away from her.

"What time is it?" Sheila mutters, letting go of the pillow.

"Seven in the morning. I have coffee all set downstairs. We can go grab a bite to eat while we're out today." Kayla points out to her.

Sheila knows that she's not going to stop badgering her about getting up. So, she throws the sheet off her and puts her feet on the bedroom floor.

"Let me guess. You have Alex's clothes bagged up and ready to go?" Sheila asks her.

"I do." Kayla laughs again as she walks out the door.

By the time Sheila gets downstairs, she can see that the bags are by the front door. There's a mug of coffee for her waiting on the counter.

"I don't want to stay here. It's gorgeous out." Kayla tells her, opening the front door and bringing the bags out to the car.

Sheila hurries to make her coffee with a small smile on her face. She can't believe how much energy that Kayla has.

She wasn't this energetic to do things in the first week. Sheila wonders if Kayla's good mood is because of how they've been with each other over the weekend.

She's not going to second guess it. She just feels the smile growing wider across her face. Happy to be a part of it all. Glad that she's there living a life that she never thought that she could have until Alex had gone with his father.

Getting into the car as Kayla locks up the house, she sees that the skies are blue. It's a little chilly out. Besides that, everything is good.

Kayla drives into town with the music up while Sheila sips at her coffee. She notices the smile on Kayla's face slowly begins to fade when they pull into the laundry mat.

"What's the matter?" Sheila asks her.

"I guess I'm not the only one that wants to do laundry on a Sunday," Kayla mutters, thinking about going to a different one.

She knows that the next laundry mat is in the next town. She doesn't have time for all of that. She doesn't want to waste her day away in a hot, humid, laundry facility just to avoid someone.

"Why?" Sheila asks, looking around the parking lot.

"Ted's here." Kayla sighs.

"It'll be all right. You don't have much laundry. We don't have to stay while we fill the washers." Sheila smiles at her.

She doesn't want Kayla to avoid him. Sheila doesn't want Kayla to act like she's not allowed to be there when she is.

Kayla shuts the car off.

"Ready for this?" Kayla sighs, looking over at Sheila.

"I was born ready. Let's get this done." Sheila winks at her and is happy that Ted's there in hopes that she will be able to see Alex.

She pictures herself walking in and seeing Alex looking at the washers bored out of his mind until he sees her, and his mother walks into the laundry mat.

It doesn't go as planned. When they go in with the bag of clothes, she doesn't see Alex anywhere.

She frowns at the idea, wondering where he is if he's not with his father.

"Good morning, I guess I wasn't the only one with the bright idea to get a head start on the week." Ted laughs and looks over at Kayla.

His smile falters just a little when he sees that Sheila is right there with her.

The Nanny.

He doesn't like that she has a smile on her face, that she seems happy. He knows that something is going on between them and he's not sure that he likes the fact that Kayla is all smiles, her eyes are beaming with happiness.

"You know me. Always wanting to get a head start." Kayla tells him, taking the washers that are by him because those are the only ones left.

"Yeah. I left before everyone woke up this morning. Linda and Alex are still sleeping. We had a campout last night. So, that was fun." Ted talks about how the weekend's going so far with their son.

"That's good. I'm glad Ted has fun with her." Kayla nods her head, not wanting to talk about anything else.

"So, how are things going between the two of you?" Ted looks over at Sheila, who's by the soda machine.

"Good, I think she's a good fit for Alex. She looks bored without him around," Kayla tells him, stuffing the washers and taking quarters out of her purse.

"You know, Kayla. It's not hard to see that you've been happier since Friday night when I picked up Alex," Ted whispers to her.

"What I do on my time without Alex, there is none of your business. I think that we've been through this." Kayla clears her throat, feeling her face growing red.

"You can't tell me nothing is going on between the two of you. You better watch out and make sure Sheila doesn't run off like the last one." Ted warns her, laughing a little.

"You know, you think that I can't hear what you're saying to her, but I can." Sheila points out to him, grabbing her soda as soon as it falls from the vending machine.

Kayla closes her eyes. When she opens them, Sheila is right there beside her, putting the soap into the machine.

"I didn't think that I was having a private conversation. I am sure that you heard." Ted spat back at her, glaring at her.

"You're just mad because she's happy. You're happy with this, Linda, right?" Sheila asks him.

"It's all right, Sheila," Kayla tells her.

"No, it's not. That's why he thinks he has the right to talk to you the way he does. If you're happy with Linda and Kayla's happy too then, I think you should just let it be. I enjoy spending time with Alex. He's a good kid. I'm his nanny while she works. If you have a problem with that, maybe you should take it up with instead of her." Sheila points her finger at him.

# Chapter Seven

"I'm just trying to make sure that she doesn't get hurt. Have you heard about the last one? The one that she thought she was going to be with after me? She had all these dreams that her life was going to be happy. It was going to be good. It seems her lover loved dick more than she liked Kayla. All I'm doing is looking out for my family." He glares at her.

"I understand that, but what you don't understand is that I'm not like any other female. I don't sit here and see what's good for me. Then when I get bored, I leave. That's not how I work. I know that there's a child involved. I know that hie and I have a bond that continues to grow. I'm getting to know Kayla on a personal level, and I know what that entails. So just leave her alone." Sheila's voice rises just a little.

Kayla doesn't know what to say. She's never had someone stick up for her like Sheila's doing now. Never had someone bold enough to take her side when she didn't even ask for help.

Ted never stuck up for her when they were together against the men that would catcall her. They would look at her as if she were a piece of meat. It didn't matter how many times she said she felt uncomfortable around them. Ted was indifferent.

Ted doesn't say anything to her. His jaw is clenching. Kayla knows what that means. It means that he doesn't know what to say. He never thought that someone would stick up for her, that someone would want to defend her in any way.

Kayla and Sheila walk out of the laundry mat when they have all the clothes in the washer. He pushes his head against the machine he's at.

Ted doesn't know why he keeps pestering Kayla about the past. Whatever happened should stay there, and he knows this.

That's why Alex loves both of them so much.

Neither of them argues in front of him. They don't make slams toward each other. They keep the conversation about the most important person.

Alex.

Ted sees them as they sit out in the car. He feels terrible for how he treated Kayla. He didn't think Sheila had heard him.

Sheila was right about that.

Ted just didn't want Alex getting in the mix of things when it went south. He takes a deep breath and lets it out slowly as he sits on the laundry table. He watches his clothes until the buzzer goes off. Then, he switches them into the dryer across the way.

Ted knows that he can't continue to badger Kayla. It's been well over a year now that anything had happened between them. He had moved on to Linda. He was happy with her, more content than he'd ever been with Kayla.

It was time for Kayla to be happy. He just wouldn't be able to stand the hurt in her eyes when things ended.

"Try to stay positive," Ted mutters to himself as he watches the two get out of the car and come back inside.

"I would've switched them over for you," Ted tells her nicely.

"Thanks, but I can do my laundry." Kayla points out to him.

Ted wants to say that he's sorry, but he can't find the words. Kayla doesn't even look at him. Neither does Sheila.

When they leave again, Sheila is thankful that the laundry is almost done. She doesn't like Kayla feeling uneasy.

"I'm sorry that I spoke out of turn like that, but he didn't have to treat you that way. I wasn't going to say anything until the last words he spoke. I just couldn't keep my mouth shut." Sheila tells her, wondering if Kayla is mad at her.

Kayla hasn't said anything to her since she and Ted had words.

"I'm not mad at you. No one has ever defended me like that. I'm shocked, I guess." Kayla points out to her.

"Really? No one?" Sheila asks, a little shocked.

"No one. I promise you that I'm not used to what you did in there." Kayla gives a small smile, and her face is tinted red.

"Well, the ones that I care about I stick up for. I mean, if it were a stranger, I don't know think that I would've said anything at all." Sheila smiles at her.

Ted gets his clothes and bags them up, going out to his car just a few spots down from Kayla's. He doesn't look or talk to them.

"It's the first time that I think anyone has put Ted in his place. He's always had something to say. Always needing the last word." Kayla laughs when they watch him pull out of his parking spot.

"Do you and Linda get along?" Sheila asks her.

"We don't talk to each other. Sometimes Linda will pick Alex up or drop him off depending on whether Ted is working late, or if he's busy doing something." Kayla shrugs one shoulder.

She's never had a problem with Linda. It isn't like Ted had left her for another woman. He had just left Kayla because she had been unfaithful.

Kayla wishes that she could take it back from time to time. She knows that no one deserves to be cheated on, but she was lonely, upset and mad. He never made time for her. When she found someone who felt the same way, it just happened to be another woman.

"How did he meet Linda?" Sheila asks when they head back into the laundry mat to get their dried clothing.

"A friend of his hooked him up with her. That's all Ted would tell me, and I've met her a few times before they became official. She's divorced, has a house, that's where Ted lives is with her. It's not like they went out and bought the house together. I just hope that if anything goes wrong between the two of them that Alex doesn't get hurt. That's the main thing between us." Kayla begins to fold her clothing before putting them back into bags.

Sheila helps her. They don't talk to each other as they continue to fold the clothes. Kayla likes to separate her clothes from Alex's so that it's easier to put away when they get back to the house.

"Does Alex come home tomorrow morning or tomorrow night?" Sheila asks.

"Tomorrow night, it gives me all day to get to work. Then, when he gets home, all my time is for him." Kayla had been thinking about it.

"That's good. It means that you're taking the time out that you need. The break that we've been talking about." Sheila tells her, grinning from ear to ear.

"Yes, did you think that I wasn't going to do what I said?" Kayla asks her.

"Some just talk. I'm just saying that I like the idea that you're sticking to this schedule that you want." Sheila laughs at her, putting the folded clothing into the bag and tying it.

They bring the bags outside to the car. Sheila is glad that they've gotten the laundry done quickly.

It's not even ten in the morning yet. But, they're heading back to the house to get the laundry put away.

Kayla gives her the bags that belong to Alex. She goes into his room. She makes sure that the folded clothes go into the designated drawers.

Sheila can't stop thinking about the hurtful look on Kayla's face when Ted was talking to her. She wished that she could've just taken Kayla into her arms and hold her tightly.

Kayla thinks that she can hide the pain behind her smile, but Sheila knows better. She's been watching Kayla. Kayla can't hide anything from her.

She hears Kayla hollering in her bed. Her heart leaps into her chest. Sheila listens for another voice, but there isn't one.

It means that Kayla's on the phone with someone that's not being nice to her. Sheila doesn't want to interrupt, knowing that it has nothing to do with her.

If Kayla wants her, then she will call for her.

It's then that she realizes that she's hollering on the phone at Ted. She can't exactly tell what's going on, but it's an argument about Alex.

She hears Kayla cry out and then something smashing against the wall of her bedroom. That's when Sheila leaves Alex's room and goes into her room to see what's going on.

Kayla's cell phone is on the floor, smashed into pieces. She can see that Kayla is crying and shaking out of anger.

"What's going on?" Sheila asks her.

"That was Ted. He doesn't think that I'm making good choices around Alex. He thinks that Alex should stay with him for a little while." She sighs.

"Can he do that? Legally?" Sheila sucks in her breath, feeling her heart pounding hard against her chest.

"No, he has to take me to court. There's no way that he can just keep Alex from me. I know this, he knows this he's just being a jerk." Kayla covers her face.

Sheila walks over to her and holds her in her arms.

"Do you want me to leave? I can if you want me to." Sheila tells her.

"I can't have you leave. There's no one that's going to watch Alex on such short notice if we do that. Ted can't do anything about how I feel about someone else. I just knew that him being quiet wasn't going to be good for me in the end." She shakes her head. Sheila holds her tighter.

She lets Kayla cry until she can't cry anymore and sees how tired she is.

"You should take a nap," Sheila suggests guiding her to the bed. Kayla lays down, letting Sheila cover her up like a mother would a child.

"Where are you going?" Kayla asks.

"Nowhere, I'm going to stay right here until you fall asleep. I will be around the house most of the day." Sheila whispers to her, kissing the side of her head.

It doesn't take long for Kayla to close her eyes. To be swept into the sleep that's awaiting her. Sheila had no plans for what she was going to do next.

She just did it.

Going out of the house and taking the car keys from the hook by the door, she gets into Kayla's car and leaves the house.

Sheila fumbles with the addresses in Kayla's GPS. Then,  she sees the one that she's looking for — Ted's address.

Either this is going to help Kayla. Or, it's going to sink her. However, that's one thing that Sheila isn't willing to let happen.

She's furious as she heads toward Ted's house. She doesn't like that Ted could play games like this. Not with Alex.

It's supposed to be about Alex. It's not about Ted or how he feels about what's going on.

She pulls into the driveway and sees that Ted's car is there at the house. She sees Ted and Alex playing catch with a football. Ted looks up, his smile fading from his face when he sees that it's Sheila and not Kayla who's come into his driveway.

"Hey, why don't you go into the house for a little bit while Daddy talks," Ted suggests when Alex looks over his shoulder and sees Sheila.

Alex doesn't listen to him and runs over to the car to hug her.

"I didn't know that you were coming over to visit today." Alex cries out, slinging his arms around her.

"I didn't know that I was going to either. It's a surprise for both of us." Sheila laughs. When Alex lets go of her, he heads into the house like Ted has asked him to do.

"What are you doing here?" Ted asks her, his smile leaving the second that Alex goes into the house.

"I think you know." Sheila glares at him, her heart pounding. She reminds herself that she has to pick and choose her words wisely, or she's going to make things worse for Kayla instead of better.

# Chapter Eight

"Look, if it's about Kayla. You have to understand where I'm coming from. Actually, you don't have to understand anything. This has nothing to do with you." Ted shakes his head as he turns his back on her.

Sheila walks toward him, walking beside him when he goes around the side of the house.

"This does concern me. You do know that there's nothing that you can do about Kayla and me being together if that's what she wants. You can't sit there and tell her that she's not going to get her kid back because I'm there. That's not okay, and you know it. No judge is going to sit there and take your side over this," Sheila tells him.

"I don't need Kayla and Alex getting hurt." Ted shakes his head.

"You don't want them to get hurt, but you're the one that's going to hurt them in the end. Alex is going to cry when he's not home tomorrow night, like his normal routine. He's going to be upset that he doesn't see his mother, that he doesn't see me." Sheila tells him, stopping him in his tracks.

"You think that this is easy for me?" Ted asks her, looking into her eyes this time.

"It should be if you want Kayla to be happy. If you want your son to be happy, then you won't do this. You're going about the past and how Kayla hurt you. Now, you want to do the same thing to her. That's not fair," Sheila whispers to him.

Her heart aches for Alex, who has no idea what's going on. Her heart aches for Kayla, who doesn't even know she's there.

"Do you know what she did after she got off the phone with you?" Sheila asks him.

"No, I can't say that I do," he mutters, going to the back porch and sitting in one of the chairs looking out over the woods that leads to a pond.

They can see it quite clearly with the leaves falling off the trees.

"She was crying. I was going to leave to make it easier on her. Not for me. It wouldn't be easy on me saying goodbye to Alex. Saying goodbye to her. I want her to be happy too, and if that means that I have to leave, then you just tell me right now. I want her to have her son." Sheila points out to him, looking at him as his eyes continue to stare off into the woods.

"I can see that Alex likes you. I didn't know that he liked you that much until he ran up to you. I'm just upset is all," Ted grunts, nodding his head.

"About what? You're the one who left her. She didn't leave you. She might have messed up, but that was on you to leave instead of working things out with her." Sheila reminds him.

Ted winces in pain but doesn't say anything about it.

"What are you so upset about?" Sheila asks him again.

"The fact that she would have the nerve to do that to me. To think that she wanted a family with me, knowing that we would make it great if she had just told me that she was into women too. I would've gone with that I would've allowed that to happen. Instead, she wanted to cheat on me. She messed everything up." Ted looks over at Sheila this time. She can see the hurt in his eyes.

"Just because you're still mad doesn't mean that you should take it out on Alex. He's a good kid because of the both of you. The way you co-parent. I don't know any parents who can do it so easily," Sheila mutters.

"No?" Ted raises his eyebrows.

"No, my parents never made it easy when they got divorced — always fighting over me, making sure that the other one has more time with me. It was horrible for me. I grew up not liking either one of them. Do you want Alex to grow up not liking you because of this stunt that you're trying to pull?" She whispers to him.

It's quiet between the two of them. Sheila hears the birds chirping and talking to one another as they fly from tree to tree.

The breeze is picking up, but she's not so cold that she wants to leave. She wants an answer from Ted. That's all she wants.

"No, I don't want him hating me. We have a great relationship. I wouldn't want to ruin that." He sighs.

"Then you need to tell her that you're not going to take her son from her because I'm there. The only thing that you can go on is that you don't' know me. Neither of us thought that something romantic was going to happen between us. We didn't even get to know each other until Alex left for the weekend. She's a hard-working mother. She tries to do everything she can for that little boy in there. Sometimes she works too hard, but it's all for him." She points toward the back door.

"That was one of her problems, always working too hard. Falling in love too hard." He adds.

"There was a time that you didn't know Linda. How did Kayla react to that?" Sheila raises her eyebrows.

"She took it with ease — one step at a time. Her track record isn't good, Sheila. It's not," Ted sighs.

"Then let her make up for the mistakes that she has made. I can't promise that she and I are going to be together forever. We're taking it day by day. I can assure you that I'm not going to hurt her. I'm not going to hurt Alex. You need to stop making her feel like she's not doing a good enough job. I could see it today at the laundry mat. How you acted toward her, I wouldn't have allowed anyone to act like that toward another human being." Sheila groans, rolling her eyes.

"I do apologize for that." Ted rubs at the wrinkles in his forehead.

"Did you tell her that?" Sheila sits back in the chair.

"No, I guess I should've." He shrugs.

"You wouldn't do that with Alex right there," Sheila tells him.

"How do you know?" Ted challenges her.

"Friday night, when you picked him up, I didn't like you. The way you talked to Kayla. At the same time, you made sure that Alex didn't hear a word that you said to her. That you waited until he was out of earshot. No matter what you say about each other, it's not done in front of Alex. That's how I know," Sheila explains to him.

"I'm sorry that we got off on the wrong foot. I shouldn't have come off like that." He mutters, and they hear the back door open.

"Who's this?" The woman at the door asks quietly.

"Alex's nanny." He tells her with no hesitation.

"My name's Sheila." She introduces herself.

"Linda, it's nice to meet you. I do have to say that he's talked a lot about you. I thought Kayla was here. I saw her car out in the driveway." Linda smiles at the two of them.

Linda has long, brown hair, her brown eyes are dark, the smile on her face lets Sheila know that she has no clue what's going on.

"It's nice to meet you. I'm glad that Alex can talk about me here. All good things I hope." Sheila laughs.

"Yes, there's no doubt in my mind that he loves you." Linda grins at her before going back into the house.

"On that note. I think that I'm going to go back to the house and make sure that Kayla's all right. She took a nap. Doesn't even know that I'm here. I didn't think that I was going to come over myself, but the emotional upset bothered me. I don't ever want to see Alex get hurt. Ted, we're on the same page whether we like each other or not." Sheila shrugs her shoulders at him and steps off the porch.

She goes around to the front of the house. Alex runs out to give her another hug. She hugs him tightly.

"I will see you tomorrow night," Alex tells her happily.

"You can count on that. We can't stay up too late." Sheila laughs at him and watches as he goes back into the house before she gets into the car and drives off.

Ted is still out in the backyard, thinking over what Sheila had said to him. He knows that his anger gets the best of him from time to time. Having someone come to him and point out what he's doing is wrong is a big step.

No one that Kayla had ever dated had been like that toward him. He knew that they weren't real from the start.

No one would want to see Kayla that upset and not do anything about it. He smiles as he looks out into the woods again.

"Do you want to go looking to see if there are any frogs out there in the pond?" Ted hears Alex calling from the back door.

"I don't think there is but get your boots on. We'll go check. We might find other things in the pond." Ted tells him, getting up from the chair.

Fall is definitely here, and he knows that the pond is going to freeze over soon. There was a thin layer across it earlier in the morning. He knows how much Alex likes going to the pond to find new things, whether it's just sticks and branches or frogs.

They won't be able to do that for much longer when winter decides to set in.

Ted watches the birds as they cluster together on the bare tree branches while he waits for Alex to come out of the house.

He sighs, knowing that Sheila's right. He can't tell Kayla that he's not bringing their son home. He knows that Linda would be upset that he would even suggest a thing like that.

He's lucky that Sheila hadn't come in hollering and screaming at him, then Linda would've known what he had said to Kayla.

Linda tries to keep to herself. She tries not to get into what she sees as their disagreements because, in the end, everything works out. Ted has to admit that this is going to blow over too. He's the one who started it, not Kayla.

"Ready?" Alex asks when he steps out of the house, closing the door behind him.

"I'm ready. Do you do this at Mom's too?" Ted asks.

"We have a pond, but it's beyond the field. You know that. You've taken me. I don't go there much anymore. I haven't shown Sheila the pond. I don't think that she'd like to touch things like frogs." He wrinkles his nose.

"You never know, you should ask her. I'm sure that she will surprise you." Ted laughs at the thought.

Alex leads the way a few feet into the woods until they come to the pond. Then, he waits for Ted, takes his hand as they circle it slowly, bend down to pick up a stray leaf, a branch, a piece of bark.

Alex likes to examine everything before he puts it back down on the ground. That's why it takes a little over an hour before they make it completely around.

There are no frogs to be seen. Alex goes into the house once he knows for a fact that he's not missing out on anything that mother nature has to offer him.

# Chapter Nine

When Sheila gets back to the house, she sees that Kayla is already up from her nap and waiting by the front door when she gets back.

"Where have you been?" Kayla asks, her eyes accusing her of doing something wrong.

"I went to go talk to Ted." Sheila sighs, feeling her heart racing as she puts the key to the car back on the hook.

"You think that you can just save everyone, don't you?" Kayla asks, rolling her eyes and turning her back on her.

"I wasn't thinking of saving anyone. I was doing what was right. I went over there and talked to Ted about what he had said to you on the phone. I don't think that it was right that he would throw Alex in the middle of this." Sheila tells her.

"I don't think that he was going to go through with it. I was upset, mad, crying. I don't think that Ted would ever do anything like that." Kayla's voice is a little rougher than before.

"I'm not going to apologize for something I felt in my heart was right. I think that we cleared up a lot of things. Now all you have to do is find another phone," Sheila tells her.

"What do you mean you've cleared up a lot of things?" Kayla whips around to face her, narrowing her eyes at her.

"Calm down. It's not like I went and screamed at Ted. He told Alex to go into the house. But, before he did, Alex hugged me. It felt so good to get a hug from him." Sheila tries to point out all the good things that had happened while she was there.

"You can't just go do things like that. How did you get Ted's address?" She puts a hand on her hip and walks into the kitchen.

"I didn't know where he lived. So, I just looked it up in your GPS," Sheila simply told her, following Kayla into the kitchen.

"Only someone who's crazy would do something like that, Sheila. Someone whose completely insane." She rolls her eyes.

"Okay, so I'm completely crazy over you," Sheila whispers to her. She wraps her arms around Kayla as she rests her hands on the counter.

"You just can't..." Kayla lets her words trail off. Sheila moves her hair to the side and slowly begins kissing the side of her neck.

"I can't what?" Sheila whispers against her ear.

"You can't do that stuff again," Kayla whispers to her, feeling Sheila's hands come around her and slowly slide up her hips, letting them settle underneath her breasts.

"What else can't I do?" She nibbles on the side of Kayla's neck, her breathing turning Kayla on more and more.

"You can do anything else that you want." She gasps, feeling the roundness of her nipples getting harder and harder.

"Good, I'm glad that you clarified all that for me." Sheila moans against the back of her ear and starts petting her through the thin shirt that she's wearing.

Kayla turns around to face her. There's a smile on her face.

"You do know how to make everything better, don't you?" Kayla asks her and feels Sheila pressing her lips against hers.

"I want you to remember how this feels during the week. I want to know how crazy you're going to become yourself without me touching you like this." Sheila slips her tongue between Kayla's welcoming lips.

Kayla whimpers for her, putting her hands around the back of Sheila's neck and pulling her in closer, grinding against her, trying not to leave an inch between them.

"Damn." Sheila moans and slowly brings her hand under and up Kayla's shirt. She is rubbing the roundness of her breasts.

Kayla pulls away from her and slowly gets out of her clothing. Sheila loves the way she looks naked. Loves that her breasts are young and perky. The way her mound looks between her legs and knowing that she's going to have that sweet bud between them.

"I want you. How I want you so much," Sheila murmurs to her.

When Kayla is done shedding her clothing, she goes to Sheila and gets her undressed quickly. She puts her hands on Sheila's hips and admires her nakedness.

"Let's take this upstairs." Sheila raises her eyebrows.

Kayla takes her hand and walks Sheila out of the kitchen. Instead of heading for the stairs, Sheila heads for the living room. She leads Kayla to the couch.

"Kayla." Sheila giggles at her and shakes her head.

"What, I don't want to do it in the bedroom." She tells her, sitting down on the couch and spreading her legs for Sheila.

Sheila's eyes go straight down the bud that she's been thinking about, that she's been wanting to taste.

She hits her knees and brings her mouth to it, suckling at it, licking and nibbling on it, making the bud grow harder.

"Yes, God, this is what I've needed." Kayla moans to her, licking her lips and running a hand through Sheila's hair as she pushes her head back against the cushions of the couch.

Sheila looks up at her. She sees that Kayla is enjoying herself. She loves the fact that Kayla can just let herself go.

She brings her mouth up from between Kayla's lips and watches as she opens her eyes.

"Why did you stop?" She gasps, biting down on her lip.

"I don't think that there's enough room on that couch to please each other." Sheila giggles at her.

Kayla blushes. Instead of standing up from the couch to move herself, she slides down until her ass is on the carpet. Then, she scooches down even further until her head is on the floor.

She spreads her legs wider and holds out her arms for Sheila.

Sheila can't resist her as she makes her to her, she kisses her softly feeling Kayla's arms go to her hips.

"Get on top of me." Kayla pleads with her, pressing her mouth harder against Sheila's.

Sheila giggles at her and nods her head, she presses her body against Kayla's and feels their nubs touching each other.

She gasps and begins to grind her body against Kayla's. With every whimper that comes out of her mouth, Kayla kisses her even harder.

They hold each other tightly, not wanting to let the other go. Kayla knows that she's found the one who she wants to be with.

She knows where she wants to be in life. Right now, she wants to be in Kayla's arms.

Sheila grinds her body until their buds are touching one another. She feels them swelling against each other. Sheila knows that it's not going to be long before they are showing each other just how much they are turned on.

"Keep going. Keep going." Kayla whimpers against her mouth, spreading her legs a little wider. Sheila can feel Kayla's legs shaking.

"I'm not going to stop until I get what I want from you," Sheila assures her and finds herself sliding up and down Kayla's body.

"Yes, just like that!" Kayla cries out, pulling her mouth away from hers.

"I know how you like it. I've known how you like it since the first time. I love that I can make your body shake. That I can show you how much I want you." Sheila whispers against her ear, sliding her body up and down hers faster and faster.

Kayla feels her breasts slightly bouncing as Sheila continues to rub her body up and down. She knows that Sheila is falling for her, and deep down, she knows that she's falling for Sheila too. She can't believe that she's found someone for her, that she's finally found someone that's not going to run away at the first sign of trouble.

"God, this feels so good," Kayla gasps at her and closes her eyes, feeling the wetness that Sheila has taken from her.

"Keep going, baby, keep going," Sheila whispers to her, needing her sweet juice to keep flowing.

Sheila doesn't know how much longer she can hold on, but it feels so good to have Kayla shaking as she holds her tightly.

"I want this. I want it all." Kayla whines at her.

"You will, everything that you want you're going to get. You deserve all the good things." She moans as she presses her mouth against Kayla's again.

She feels herself cumming with Kayla, The gates have opened up. She's not holding anything back from her.

Kayla's eyes grow wide feeling Sheila's body submit to hers. It feels so good that they can come together like this.

When they're done, they're breathless. Sheila doesn't get off her. Kayla holds her tightly with a big smile on her face.

"I didn't think that this was going to happen today. To be honest, I thought that we were going to be fighting." Sheila giggles against her mouth.

"I was upset when you left, I had a feeling I knew where you went, but I wasn't sure. I don't like that people use my car, but this time it was all right. You didn't know." Kayla smiles at her.

Sheila finally moves from Kayla when she feels the coolness coming in through the window that she didn't know was open.

"You think that anyone heard us?" Sheila laughs, nodding her head toward the window.

"I don't care if they did. I'm allowed to do what I want in my own home." Kayla laughs at her, sitting up and pressing her back against the couch.

"That was truly amazing. I love that you want me so much." She whispers to her, kissing her again before she stands up on her feet.

"Where are you going?" Kayla asks her, watching her head out of the living room.

"I'm going to get our clothes, put them in the hamper. Then, I'm going to take a shower. I nice, hot shower. Unless you want to join me." Sheila winks at her.

"Maybe next time." Kayla laughs, getting to her feet and heading up the stairs to get something on.

Kayla throws a robe on the second she gets into her room. She goes to her bedroom window. She can't believe that a year ago, she was heartbroken, thinking that she could trust no one. Now Sheila is in her life . She feels like she can trust her with anything that goes on.

It helps that Sheila is more than willing to stick up for her. She's more than happy to defend her and Alex both.

Sheila had promised that she would do her best to show her love for Kayla. She was doing just like she had promised.

She goes to her desk and takes out a notebook and pen. Sheila starts to write out the days of the week and the time that she's going to start working, her breaks, and the time that she finishes work. It takes a little bit. When she's happy with it, she transfers the schedule to the whiteboard that she has hung over her desk.

When she gets up from the chair, she can see that Sheila is standing in the doorway.

"Where are you going with that?" she asks.

"I'm going to take it into my office so that I can hang it up on the wall. I have the schedule all planned out, and I'm going to stick to it." Kayla nods her head firmly.

"I'm so proud of you. I know that Alex is going to be happy when he sees it. Knowing that you're trying to spend more time with him." Sheila beams with pride.

"More time for the two of you," Kayla tells her, kissing her on the mouth quickly before she leaves the room.

# Chapter Ten

Sheila loves the way that Kayla corrects her. She hadn't thought much about herself. She felt that she would have time with Kayla when Alex was in bed.

The more time they spend together, the more she knows that Kayla isn't going to act like they're friends in front of Alex. It's a sign that Kayla believes that she's not going anywhere. The trust that she feels between them makes Sheila's heart melt.

It's late in the evening when Sheila finally goes to her room. Not that she wants to, but Kayla is tossing and turning through the night.

She imagines how it's going to be when they are sharing a room. Sheila wondered if Kayla would be upset to find that she left Kayla's bed.

It's almost three in the morning. Sheila's almost asleep when she hears her bedroom door opening.

"Why didn't you stay?" Kayla asks her softly.

"I couldn't sleep with you moving around like you were thrashing in the middle of the ocean." Sheila points out to her.

"I'm sorry. Sometimes I have these horrible dreams. I woke up, and you weren't there, which made it worse," Kayla confesses to Sheila.

Sheila moves over so that Kayla can lay down with her. She cuddles her into her arms, tightens her grip around Kayla.

"I'm not going anywhere. What were you dreaming about?" Sheila dares to ask her.

"You were gone, you left without even leaving a note. I woke up one morning. All your things were gone. Alex came in and asked where you were. We searched the house from top to bottom. But, there was no sign of you. And, Ted was in my dream," Kayla shutters at the thought.

"Why?" Sheila sucks in her breath.

"I thought that maybe you'd gone over there. When Ted realized that you had just up and left, he laughed at me. Telling me that no one wanted to stay with me. Telling me that I had been wrong again about the love of my life." Kayla whimpers at her, feeling the tears coming to her eyes, feeling her body sweating again.

"Kayla, that's not going to happen. I'm not going to let it happen." Sheila shushes her and runs a hand through her hair.

"I hope not. I mean, things are going great between us. I don't know why I would have such a horrible dream." She shakes her head, clinging to Sheila.

"Maybe because it's always happened to you before. I know that you're scared that I'm going to leave. I wouldn't do that to you. Even if I were going to, I would let you know. I wouldn't just leave in the middle of the night." Sheila shakes her head back and forth.

"You promise?" Kayla asks.

"Yes, I promise you. That's not who I am. That's not who I'm going to be. There's so much more to you than what meets the eye. The others didn't want to stick around to see it. They don't know what they've lost, but I know what I've gained." Sheila admits to her.

Kayla feels a smile come to her face as she drifts back off to sleep.

Sheila doesn't go back to sleep. She continues to hold Kayla in her arms. She feels sad that Kayla would have to think things like that.

All the others had hurt her, had made her feel unwanted and abandoned. Sheila knows that she won't do the same thing to her.

If she has to prove it to Kayla time, and again she will. She knows that Kayla needs reassurance because of the ones that have hurt her.

She knows that it's not Kayla's fault for feeling this way. Sheila also knows she's going to have to prove to Kayla and probably Alex that she's going to be there for a long time. Hopefully forever.

Sheila thinks about her trips around the world that she wants to take. She sees them going together. Sheila knows it would take a long time to convince Kayla. In the end, she's sure that she would be able to.

It could be a summer trip. Sheila wouldn't have to say goodbye. They would come back home in the fall. Then, Kayla would be satisfied knowing that the love of her life went with her and the boy that she's grown to love as well.

"I won't ever abandon you," Sheila whispers to her.

The only response she gets is a deep sigh from Kayla while she's sleeping. Sheila feels that it's good enough for her.

Sheila's just happy that Kayla can now sleep in comfort until the alarm goes off at six in the morning.

Sheila is tired when Kayla wakes up. Kayla feels terrible for keeping her up all night. She knew that it was just a dream, and it wasn't going to happen.

"I am sorry," Kayla whispers to her.

"There's no reason to be sorry. I know how it feels not to be wanted. Maybe not as much as you have, but I know the feeling." Sheila yawns and gets off the bed as soon as Kayla gets up.

"I'm going to get to work. I'm already ten minutes late." Kayla tells her, walking out of the room.

"I'll start the coffee and bring a cup up to you!" Sheila calls after her. She feels a smile come to her face when she hears Kayla giggling down the hall.

That's the only thing she wants to hear in the house. The laughter that Kayla has missed out on for so long.

She does exactly what she plans to and watches the coffee brew. Though it seems to take forever, she makes the coffee quickly. When the beeping goes off, Sheila knows it's ready.

Bringing up the coffee mug, she stands in the doorway of the office. She sees how Kayla works intently at the computer. She has a headset on so that she can talk to clients without having to press an ear to her phone, helping them through the computer at the same time.

Kayla looks over at her and smiles. Sheila walks into the room and places the coffee mug down in front of her.

"You should also find some time to eat," Sheila whispers to her, walking out of the room and leaving her alone the rest of the day.

Sheila goes room to room, not wanting to work out. She goes in and out of Alex's room. She goes outside to the pool. Although it's sunny outside, it's too cold to go swimming. She pouts, knowing that she can't bother Kayla because she's working.

It's not long before Kayla comes downstairs to take a break. She sees that Sheila is sitting at the kitchen table.

"Why do you look so upset?" Kayla laughs at her, kissing her on the cheek.

"I'm bored. I have no one to play with. You're working, and Alex isn't back yet." Sheila sighs, shaking her head.

"You're going to make it, I promise." She laughs again. It feels good that Sheila misses her already because the weekend is over. Now it's time to get back down to business.

"I know, I just don't find any enjoyment around the house without one of you guys in close contact." Sheila shrugs her shoulders.

"I will show you some close contact tonight." She giggles, kissing her again and heading back upstairs.

Sheila smiles at the thought of it. Then she hears the doorbell ringing.

She hurries away from the table to go to the door. She sees that Linda and Alex are there waiting to be let in.

"Good afternoon." Sheila smiles at both of them.

"Hi. Alex has already had a shower. He has clean clothes on and should be ready for bed tonight. He's been running around most of the day outside in the woods with Ted. He's eaten a late lunch." She goes on to tell about how his days been.

Sheila nods her head as Alex runs through the house. Linda hands her the overnight bag that he'd left with.

"Just between you and me, I think if you're not going to take this seriously with Kayla and Alex, then you should leave now. I'm not trying to be mean about it. They've had some hard times." Linda whispers to her.

"Just between you and me, I'm not going anywhere." Sheila winks at her, and they laugh together.

"That's good to know. When I saw you over yesterday morning, I thought that you were letting Ted know that you couldn't be Alex's nanny anymore. Then he came to me about what was going on. We got into an argument. Not in front of Alex, but it was still heated. I can't believe he'd say something like that. Ted has a lot of issues. I'm glad that I'm here for them both. Sometimes Ted is so sweet. Other times, it's all about him. No matter what, in the end, he always comes out with what he's done. He's stupid sometimes." She rolls her eyes at the thought of it.

"All men are. Sometimes we make mistakes, and we learn from them. I'm glad that he hasn't done anything that's going to hurt Alex's feelings." Sheila points out.

"That's why he's home. He's dumb to think that I would allow him to do such a thing. I hope you guys have a good day." Linda tells her, waving and heading back to her car.

Sheila stays in the doorway until Linda gets into her car. Then she waves to her one last time.

"Do you want to go out and play in the leaves?" Sheila asks Alex when she finally can get him to settle down.

"No, I would like to watch movies and have some hot chocolate. It's getting cold out there." Alex makes a shivering motion, and Sheila laughs at him.

"It's so glad to have you home." She shakes her head and watches as he hops up in the living room chair, and getting ready to turn on the television while she goes into the kitchen and makes him hot chocolate.

Sheila gets ready to make dinner that night, and Kayla stops her.

"I think we should order take out tonight. There's no reason to heat up the stove." She grins as she comes down the stairs.

"Mom!" Alex shouts and runs to her, hugging her tightly. It makes Sheila's heart skip a beat.

"Do you want to have a movie night tonight?" Kayla asks him.

"The three of us?" he asks, looking up at her.

"Yes, the three of us." Kayla nods her head, looking over at Sheila to see if she has any plans for the evening.

"I think that would be a good idea." Sheila agrees.

"Does that mean we can bring the pillows and blankets down and campout?" he asks her, knowing that they haven't done that in a long time.

"Yes, I can't remember the last time we did that." She laughs.

"Last summer." He tells her, running away from her and stomping up the stairs to get his things.

Sheila updates Kayla about what Linda told her. Kayla orders pizzas and soda for them to have as Alex dumps his bedding on the living room floor.

He runs back upstairs for his own collection of movies that he has in the bedroom. Grabbing three or four of them, he rushes back down and puts them on the couch.

# Chapter Eleven

"If you keep running up and down the stairs like that, you're going to fall." Sheila raises her eyebrows at him.

"I haven't yet, but okay." Alex rolls his eyes at her and laughs.

By the time that they have the cushions on the floor and the sleeping bags pulled out to lie on, the doorbell rings.

Sheila goes to answer it. Kayla gets ready to pop a movie in. Coming back with three different kinds of pizza and two different options of soda, Sheila puts them down on the coffee table.

"We don't need plates," Sheila tells them, showing them the paper plates that came with the boxes of pizza.

Alex sits between Kayla and Sheila on the floor as they watch a cartoon movie first. His eyes are watching the movie intently while he shoves the pizza into his mouth.

Sheila can feel Kayla looking at her from over Alex's head. She smiles at Kayla. This is the life that she's always wanted.

Worried that she couldn't have her own children, she is now happy. Kayla is sharing Alex with her. She can picture her future with them and becoming a family like Ted and Linda.

Sheila can see how happy they are together. She's glad that Kayla wants to make the next move into this relationship that seems to be growing stronger and stronger every day.

They watch a few more movies. That's when Kayla realizes that it's after midnight. She needs to get to bed before she doesn't wake up to her alarm in the morning.

Alex is already sleeping. So, she covers him up, kisses him on the forehead before she gets up from the blankets.

"Where are you going?" Sheila whispers to her.

"I can't sleep down here. I already have my shoulders and neck aching. I don't need my complete body aching." Kayla whispers to her.

Sheila watches Kayla as she goes up the stairs . She watches the movie for a few more minutes before getting up herself.

She checks the door making sure that it's locked. Sheila makes sure that the backdoor's locked before she peeks in on Alex again.

His eyes are still closed. He's in the same position that he fell asleep in as she slowly makes her way up the stairs.

Sheila walks into the bedroom. She watches as Kayla gets undressed, closing the door behind her.

"I thought that you were going to play tonight?" Sheila whispers to her, biting down on her lip.

"I didn't realize that Alex was going to stay up so late. I thought that he was exhausted." She rolls her eyes.

"I guess Linda doesn't know him like she thinks she does." Sheila giggles and stops Kayla from putting her nightclothes on.

"Lie down on the bed. I will give you a message." Sheila tells her, remembering how tired

Kayla was from the night before, all the tossing and turning couldn't have been good for her back.

Kayla smiles at her and does what Sheila tells her to.

"You've succeeded today. Taking the breaks that you needed to, making sure that you found time for Alex," Sheila whispers to her. Then she slides out of her own clothing and makes certain the bedroom door is locked.

"I did do great." Kayla agrees with her, laying on her stomach and closing her eyes as she feels Sheila straddling her.

"Is this massage for you or for me?" Kayla teases her softly, feeling her body waking up not feeling as tired as she thought she was.

"I think it's for both of us. I missed you so much today. I couldn't wait for Alex to go to sleep myself. I was hoping that Linda was right about how tired he was, but I guess not." Sheila giggles. She then brings her hands to Kayla's shoulders.

Kayla lets her body relax as Sheila begins to rub her down with her soft hands. She can't believe how good it feels.

She can't remember the last time that she'd had a massage. She takes a deep breath and lets it out slowly.

"You're so beautiful, Kayla. Did you know that?" Sheila whispers to her, licking her lips. She runs her hands down the side of Kayla's body, bringing them to her lower back and kneading her fingers in deep.

"I didn't know that." Kayla gasps and moans. She can feel the soft touch Sheila has.

"You are so beautiful. Sexy even." Sheila moans as she feels the heat coming from between Kayla's legs.

Sheila slides her body down a little further. She feels Kayla opened her legs for than what they were before, teasing her silently.

"Why don't you show me just how sexy I am." Kayla challenges her, biting down on her lip. She feels Sheila's body on top of hers.

She can feel Sheila's hole pressing against hers. She feels the heat between them. She can feel her lips spreading under her, as her bud pressing against the sheets.

"I want to show you every night just how sexy you are. How lucky I am to have you in my life." Sheila moans against the back of her ear as she slides her hands under Kayla and fondles her breasts. Sheila touches them gently, teasing and groping at them until Kayla is whimpering for her.

"How about that? Do you like that?" Sheila moans against her ear, feeling Kayla's nubs getting hard under her fingers.

"Yes, I like it. I want it." She nods her head, grinding herself against the bed and feeling Sheila's hole bumping against her own.

"I wouldn't have it any other way. I want to please you. I want to be the one that you go to for the sexual pleasures, for the hard times in life." Sheila whispers to her, sliding her body up and down Kayla's.

Kayla closes her eyes and nods her head at her, feeling Sheila tugging at her hair playfully.

"I feel how wet you are. I love the wetness." Sheila murmurs, sliding Kayla's hair aside and licking at the back of her neck.

"Do you?" She giggles and gasps at the same time.

"I do." She grinds against Kayla's hole to show her just how much she truly enjoys it.

Kayla jumps when she feels Sheila's hand sliding down her body until her hand settles on her mound.

"Sweet, sweet, Kayla. That heat feels so good." She whines at her.

Kayla begins to grind against the fingers that are pressing against her now. She feels her hole getting wetter and wetter.

Sheila closes her eyes. She loves hearing the moaning that's coming from Kayla's mouth. She loves the way that Kayla grinds on her fingers. Sheila knows each time she does, she's closer to cumming for her.

"Stop, just stop for a second," Kayla tells her, gasping out the words.

"You don't want it?" Sheila opens her eyes and bites down on her lip.

"No, that's not it. I love it." Kayla tells her softly. She feels Sheila getting off her and moving around so that she can lay on her back to see her.

"I want to please you. You always please me, and I want to." Kayla tells her softly as she kisses Sheila on the mouth. She then moves her so that she's on her back.

Sheila whimpers as Kayla gets on top of her, not wasting any time on straddling her, she thrusts her hips, grinding her mound against Sheila's feeling their buds touching each other. She feels Sheila's hands on her breasts, feeling her legs opening wider and wider.

"Oh God," Sheila moans to her, feeling her thrusting faster and faster watching Kayla's head tilt toward the ceiling.

"I told you that I wanted to please you. That I wanted to make sure that you were satisfied too." Kayla whines at her.

"You're doing such a good job. I love this." Sheila moans to her, gripping her breasts tightly, pushing them together. Sheila looks up at Kayla when she looks down at her.

They have smiles on their faces. They're having so much fun with each other. At the same time, their feelings are just growing stronger and stronger with each thrust of Kayla's hips that continue to grind against hers.

"I'm going to make sure that you feel loved too. I wanted to make you feel loved all day. I had to work." Kayla whimpers and whines at her.

Sheila knows that Kayla is getting ready to cum for her because she's slowing down the pace of her thrusting.

Sheila lets go of her breasts, grips Kayla's hips tightly and begins to bring her back and forth. Kayla whimpers and whines at her.

"Yes, we're almost there. I can feel it. I feel your bud pulsing against mine." Sheila whimpers with her, biting down on her lip.

"I want to cum, God I want to cum with you," Kayla tells her, feeling the sweat on her forehead, feeling the wetness running down her body.

"Yes, I do too. I love this. You make me feel so good." Sheila tells her softly and pulls her even closer to her.

"Cum for me," Sheila tells her softly, her voice full of intimacy, full of love that she has for her.

Sheila can hear her panting. She can feel her getting wetter and wetter each time she thrusts her back and forth.

It's not going to be long. She feels Kayla's nails digging into her shoulders as Sheila feels her cumming.

Sheila cums with her as they moan. They together, whimpering softly for one another until Kayla is shaking. Sheila knows that she can't get her to cum anymore for her.

Kayla lies down on her, holding her tightly.

"God, that was so good, you don't even know how good that was. I can't believe how awesome it was." Kayla tells her through trying to get her breathing back to normal.

"There's more where that comes from. I'm going to stick around and show you." Sheila giggles against her ear, pushing Kayla's hair out of her face.

They hold each other for a while, even when their breathing has gone back to normal. That's when Sheila realizes that Kayla has fallen asleep on top of her.

She gently rolls her off and covers her with the sheet that's still on the bed, covering her up to her shoulders.

Sheila gets dressed and leaves the bedroom, closing the door quietly behind her. Then, she heads back downstairs.

The movie is over with. The credits are rolling as she looks in on Alex and sees that he's still sleeping.

She smiles down at him. She takes the couch, knowing that she's not going to be able to sleep on the floor without feeling it in the morning.

Taking one of the blankets off the floor, she covers herself. She keeps an eye on Alex until she falls asleep herself with a smile on her face.

It's late in the morning when she feels someone staring at her, peeking out of one eye she sees Alex staring at her.

"Good morning." She smiles at him and sits up on the couch.

"Good morning." He grins.

"How long have you been awake?" Sheila asks him.

"Long enough to go check on Mom to see that she's working. Then, come back down here to see when you were going to wake up." Alex thinks about it for a second.

"Have you eaten yet?" Sheila asks, getting up from the couch.

"Yeah, Mom made sure that I ate. I see that she has a schedule for herself." Alex tells me thinking about it for a second.

"There's a lot of things that are going to be changing around here. We're trying to make things better around here for you." Sheila hugs him and feels his arms go around her.

"I hope that you don't ever leave her," Alex tells her. Sheila hugs him even tighter.

# Chapter Twelve

Sheila can feel the love that comes off Alex. She doesn't say anything. She knows that she's not going anywhere. Kayla isn't the only one that wants her to stick around. She isn't the only one that's worried about her leaving.

"What are we going to do today while Mom's working?" Sheila asks.

"I don't know. I think perhaps we could go to the park. Mom already says that we can't go swimming anymore. She's going to have someone drain the pool until next summer." He rolls his eyes.

"Only because it's getting too cold . She doesn't want you coming down sick. We know she's only worried about you and your health." Sheila laughs at him.

"Yeah, but she has to understand there's not much to do around here either. I like that she's taking more time off, but it doesn't mean we have to stick around the house." He points out to her.

Sheila laughs at him and shakes her head.

"I like throwing the football around. We don't have one here." He tells her.

"Well, we can get that without a problem. We can go to the store." Sheila points out to him.

"Yeah?" He asks.

"Sure, go up. Tell your mom that we're going to the store, and we'll be back in a little while," Sheila tells him.

She gets upstairs and gets dressed while Alex goes to his mother. Alex comes out of the office with a smile on his face.

"Are you ready?" She asks him as they head down the stairs together.

"I'm ready," Alex tells her as they head out of the front door.

Sheila takes her own car keys and gets Alex into the backseat of the car. Sheila makes sure that he's buckled. She then gets into the driver's seat.

It's the first time that we're going together to the store to pick something up. I am happy to know that Kayla trusts me with him this much.

"Did your mom think it was surprising that we were going to head out?" Sheila asks him, looking at him in the rearview mirror.

"No, she was shocked. I think she was happy that we were getting out." Alex looks out the window onto the sidewalks as we go by the houses.

They go to the store on the outskirts of town. Sheila thinks that he's going to get something other than the football he wants.

She watches him take the ball off the shelf. They then head for the line.

"There's nothing else that you want?" she asks him.

"No, nothing that I can think of. We can throw it around out front of the house as I do with Dad." Alex tells her, that glow in his eyes.

Sheila can see that he's like a typical man. Getting what needs and that's it not wanting to waste any more time in the store.

When they get back, it's lunchtime. Kayla already has sandwiches made for them when they walk in through the door.

"I like this more and more. I get the work that I need to, done for the day and still have time in between." She grins at the two of them.

Sheila can see that she wants to go over and kiss her . She hesitates, not doing it in front of Alex. Not that Alex is paying attention, but Sheila can see the look in Kayla's eyes. The shine in them, the beam of happiness.

"I didn't think that you'd let me take him to the store," Sheila tells her the second that Alex takes his food into the living room.

"I have to trust you sooner or later out of my sight with him you brought him back in one piece." She whispers, kissing Sheila hard on the mouth like she wanted to since they had come in.

"I would never intentionally hurt him." Sheila kisses her back before pulling away from her.

"I know that I was a little anxious when Alex told me that you guys were going to get a football for him. I almost told him that I wanted to go with you guys. It wasn't that I wanted to go, but I hung back and watched how you handled it," Kayla confesses to her. Sheila giggles a little.

"It'll get easier each time we go out without you," Sheila assures her.

"I know it will. Just Alex has never gone with anyone that I've been involved with. Not so willingly. He never wanted to leave my side. I think that's one of the reasons I never got to get all the work done that I am now." Kayla blushes a little.

Sheila can see that there are a lot of new things that Kayla is going to have to get used to as well as Alex.

"Do you have time to toss the ball with us tonight after dinner?" Sheila asks, wondering just how good Kayla is doing sticking to her schedule.

"Yes, I'm going to make time for that. It's getting darker and darker now that fall is setting in." Kayla reminds her.

"We have a front porch light for a reason." Sheila points out.

She nods her head. Kayla takes a bite of the sandwich that Sheila has in her hand before she makes her way back to her office to get back to work.

"Are you ready to go out yet?" Alex asks, finishing his sandwich and getting a drink of water quickly.

"I think that you should fill a jug with water so that we don't' have to keep running in and out. We're going to work up a sweat out there." Sheila tells him.

"Good idea." He nods his head. He does what she asks him to do while she takes the football out of the package.

"I can't remember the last time I threw one of these. I like feeling young again." Sheila points out to him.

"You are young. Even Linda doesn't go out and toss the football with me. She's always in the house not that I don't like her. She just doesn't do a lot of things with me the way you do," Alex tells her as he watches the water fill the jug.

Sheila walks out of the kitchen with a huge smile on her face.

Linda doesn't look like the type that would pass the ball even if she wasn't busy. Too afraid of breaking a nail or something.

She bites down on her lip before the laughter bubbles up her throat and out of her mouth. She doesn't want Alex thinking that she's laughing at Linda.

Sheila can tell how much Alex loves her.

It's not long before Alex is outside in the front yard with her. Her arms already ache from throwing the ball a few times. However, Sheila isn't complaining. She can see the happiness on Alex's face when he throws the ball back at Linda.

"You have a good arm," Sheila tells him.

"I'm hoping that one day Mom might let me play football when I start going to school. I know that I'm good. My dad and I throw the ball all the time. He's going to ask her with me. I think that we should have a meeting and get together to talk to Mom about it when the time comes." Alex tells her the plan that he has in mind.

"You really don't think that your mother is going to let you play football?" Sheila is a little surprised at the thought of Kayla telling him no.

"She doesn't want me to get hurt. I can already hear her telling me that football is too rough." Alex mutters, rolling his eyes as he throws the ball back hard to Sheila.

She catches it and feels the stinging sensation of the ball hitting her hand. She feels how painful it is but she doesn't show it.

She laughs and tosses the ball back to him, without beaming it.

"I think that you're pretty good at throwing a ball for a girl." He laughs at her and Sheila giggles shaking her head at him.

She doesn't know how long they stay out in the front yard, but by the time that they get ready to go into the house the sun is going behind the treetops.

"That was a lot of fun." He wipes the sweat off his face.

"How about you go upstairs and get in the shower. I think that it's almost time for dinner. A nice bowl of hot soup would be good. It's so chilly out there." Sheila tells him.

"Okay, I will let Mom know that you're getting ready to cook." He tells her, stopping at the foot of the stairs.

"What's the matter?" She asks him, a little worried that he's not heading up the stairs like he'd planned to do.

"Do you know what would make this even better?" Alex asks, looking at her instead of at the top of the stairs.

"What's that?" Sheila raises her eyebrows at him.

"If you and Mom were like Dad and Linda. It would be amazing to have you as a stepparent. I don't know much about how things work, but I do know that I like having you around. I don't really see you as my nanny because you are both here with me you both are doing things with me." Alex grins from ear to ear before taking the stairs two at a time.

Sheila nods her head at the idea. She isn't going to be the one to tell Alex that they're working on becoming just that. She doesn't want to get his hopes up. If Kayla tells him, then she will be the one that's shoving this into a relationship that Sheila is ready for.

She knows that she's ready, these times with Alex with Kayla are the best that she's ever had. She can't imagine a day without them.

Hoping that he tells Kayla the same thing that he had told her downstairs, but she's not going to push it.

She hums as she gets the beef stew out from under the cupboard. She puts it in the pot on the stove.

It's not going to take long for dinner. Although it's out of a can, it will still warm their chilled bodies.

She hears Alex shut the bathroom door upstairs and then hears the water turning on. Glad that he had done what she asked.

Kayla comes down before Alex I the bathroom. Kayla looks tired.

"It's early to bed for you tonight." Sheila points out to her teasingly.

"I think it's early for bed for everyone." Kayla laughs and hugs her at the stove, putting her arms around her and just standing there.

"Today has been a great day. A wonderful day as usual." Sheila kisses the top of her head, making sure that she's listening for Alex.

"I think so. I know that Alex thinks so." Kayla tells her, letting her go so that she can get the milk and glasses to set on the dining room table.

"How do you know that?" Sheila tests the waters.

"He came to me while I was working. Letting me know that you were going to make soup for supper. He doesn't like soup." She laughs.

"Well, it's not really soup, more like beef stew." Sheila stirs it around and bites down on her lip.

"And another thing. He talked to me about how he likes the fact that you're here all the time. He gets to spend time with you. Alex tells me it's almost like at his dad's house where Linda is there helping and how they are always happy around each other. He wants the same thing here." Kayla tells her from the dining room.

"Are you going to tell him?" Sheila asks her when she walks back into the kitchen.

"I might hold off a few more days, why?" Kayla looks at her a little nervously.

"No reason, I think that it would be a good idea. Alex approves, that's for sure. If he didn't, then he wouldn't have brought it up, right?" Sheila raises her eyebrows.

"Right." She grins and gets the bowls out of the cupboard for Sheila to fill. Then, they hear Alex coming down the stairs loudly.

It's one thing that Sheila can always count on. She doesn't have to listen too carefully for when Alex is getting ready to come in and out of a room.

He naturally makes it known that he's on his way.

# Chapter Thirteen

Kayla looks at Alex. She and sees that over the past two days, he's become happier at home, coming out more with what's on his mind.

A week ago, she wouldn't have expected him to talk about the thoughts that were running through his head. The schedule that she's keeping, she knows she never would've thought of it if it wasn't for Sheila. She can't believe how much she'd been missing out on before the schedule she's been keeping herself to.

"What?" Alex asks, eating his food as if he's never eaten a day in his life.

"Nothing, I'm just watching you." Kayla laughs, embarrassed that she's gotten caught.

"You know, I expected to come home and have it be the same way it used to be. You always stuck in your office, while Sheila and I find things to entertain ourselves with, until you got done working for the day. Sometimes Sheila would be the one to tuck me in at night. I like that things are changing." Alex tells her, giving her a grin.

"Me too. Speaking of change…" She lets her voice trail off and looks at Sheila for a moment before her eyes go back to Alex.

"What?" He asks her, not sure what she's going to be talking about and he lets the fear set in while he looks at Sheila himself and then back at his mother.

"The discussion that we had upstairs." She tells him, clearing her throat.

"Look, if you don't want to that's all right. You don't have to. I just think that it's feeling more and more like Dad's house the longer I stay here. I know that you're all about me and you want me to have everything that I've ever wanted. I just want you to be happy too. I want you to feel the happiness that I feel when I wake up in the morning. I know that Sheila's going to be here. I know what my routine is. I like it." He points out to her, not exactly sure what she's going to say but he wants to be heard too.

"That's what I'm getting at. Sheila and I like each other the way Dad and Linda do." She reaches out her hand. Sheila takes it.

The smile slowly creeps across his face and he rolls his eyes at the two of them.

"What?" Kayla laughs at him.

"I don't say anything, but I see the way the two of you look at each other. I know that there's something there. I'm glad that you don't flaunt it because Dad and Linda don't, but they do show their love for each other." He sits back now that his bowl is empty.

"Well, I didn't want you thinking that things were moving too fast. I always want what's best for you no matter what." Kayla puts a hand on his shoulder so that he doesn't just walk off on her.

"I know that. I can't wait until school starts back up again. I want to join the football team." He clears his throat.

He thinks that it's the best time to talk about it since they're discussing things at the dinner table.

She sighs at him, shaking her head.

"I'm good. You have to see that. Throw the ball with me." He tells her, getting up from his chair and leaving the bowl where it is on the dining room table.

"Go on. He wants to show you. I will clean this up." Sheila winks at her. Kayla goes out after him into the dark in the front yard.

Kayla laughs when she watches Alex throw the ball to her, she's amazed at how far he can throw and the steady arm that he has.

"That's a quarterback's arm right there." She throws it back to him, but it doesn't reach him.

He goes running after the ball and is happy to see that his mother is out there with him. She might throw like a girl, but that doesn't matter. He just wants more time with her.

They stay outside for a little while longer until Kayla can't throw another ball to him.

"You're doing better than what you had in the beginning." He tells her, carrying the football under one arm.

"Yeah, well, I'm going to have to think about this football thing. I don't want you getting hurt." She points out to him.

"I told Sheila that you'd say something like that. That's such a Mom thing to say." He sighs, shaking his head.

"I didn't say no." She laughs at him as they enter the house.

Alex goes upstairs and washes up again. He goes into his room to get changed for the night. As he's pulling back the blankets to get into his bed, Kayla walks in and looks at his bookshelf.

"I'm a little too old to have bedtime stories." He grins at her, shaking his head.

"Then I will just tuck you in like I used to do," Kayla tells him a little offended that he doesn't want her reading bedtime stories anymore.

"I'm never too old for that," he tells her.

"You know, at the end of this month, you're going back to school. How's it going to feel being a second-grader?" she asks him.

"I don't know. I'm nervous. I like the fact that this summer has turned around in such a positive way. You and Dad seem to be getting along better." He shrugs his shoulders.

"I was thinking…" She bites down on her lip.

He searches her eyes, not sure what she's going to come out with next.

"I don't think that we need a meeting or anything like that. I want you to play sports if that's what you want to do. I'm not going to hold you back from the things that interest you, Alex." Kayla finds it hard to let him do this.

"Really?" he asks, excitement in his voice.

"Yes, I looked it up. Football camp has already started. Once school starts, you're going to have practices twice a week. Games are on Saturdays. I already put in the money for it. If you change your mind at any point, you can tell me that you don't like it and we can try something else next season. However, if you find you don't like it, you're still going to have to follow through with it." Kayla explains to him.

"That's great. I'm sure that I'm going to like it." He hugs her tightly to him. Kayla knows that she had made the right choice.

"I just want you to have fun. I want you to be happy. I wasn't able to do cheering. I still wonder how I would've turned out if my mother had let me." Kayla tells him lightly.

Alex lets her go. She tucks him into bed tightly before kissing him on the forehead and shutting off the lamp that he has beside his bed.

The hall light is beaming into the room. Just as she's about to close the door all the way he shakes his head.

"Leave it open a crack," he tells her softly.

She sees the redness growing on his cheeks. Kayla nods her head. He's still a child no matter how adult he sounds. She knows that the only reason he wants that door open is for a night light, he just doesn't want to tell her that.

Kayla smiles as she heads to her bedroom . She sees that Sheila is already standing there waiting for her.

"So?" Sheila asks her.

"He's so happy that we've signed him up. I think that he's going to do good. I think that he's going to break a lot of bones..." She takes a deep breath and lets it out slowly.

"I'm sure if he does, he's going to go to the hospital with a smile on his face. You can't keep him from doing things. You can't wrap him in bubble wrap and protect him from the world. Good and bad things are going to. You have to roll with the punches." Sheila tells her, pulling her in for a hug.

Kayla hugs her back tightly. She's happy that Sheila is right there with her. And, that they're doing everything together.

"You know it's not always going to be like this. We're going to get into fights. We're going to disagree about things. One thing I know for sure I'm not going to walk away from all this." Kayla tells her, holding her just a little tighter.

"Neither am I. No matter what comes our way we are going to talk, communicate about things. That's what I've always learned. Not because I was taught that. Because I learned what to do by seeing things that I don't ever want to happen in my life or to the ones that I love." Sheila whispers against her ear.

"Are you ready to be tucked in?" Kayla laughs at her.

"Yes, I'm ready whenever you are." Sheila laughs with her. She's happy that they can have a serious discussion and end it in such a loving manner.

"It's going to feel weird when he goes back to school. There's not going to be much to do around here during the hours that he's going to be gone." Sheila tells her when they get into bed together.

"What are you getting at?" Kayla asks.

"I'm getting at that I wouldn't mind getting a part-time job and helping out. I can watch Alex while you're working. I will get mother's hours or whatever they call it." Sheila shrugs her shoulders.

"You really want to do this." Kayla nods her head.

"Yes, I told you that I wanted to. I'm going to help you in all aspects. Whether it's something that Alex needs or something that you need. The bills, the rent. You shouldn't have to do this on your own." Sheila points out to her.

"Thank you," Kayla tells her, not knowing what else to say to her.

"I don't know why you're thanking me," Sheila tells her, grinning from ear to ear.

"For helping. I mean, no one has ever gone to this length. I mean Ted, sure, but he has to." She laughs lightly.

"I am going to prove to you and Alex that I'm going to be here no matter what. I will even prove it to Ted as well. It was all Alex who invited me to throw the ball around, who wanted to get the ball today. He brought us closer together when I thought I was as close as I was going to get." Sheila confesses to her.

"It means that he wants you here all the time. That's always a good thing." Kayla nods her head and turns the television on.

"It's always a good day as long as I'm here with the two of you. Just think, when I do get a job, you don't have to work all the time." Sheila points out.

"I don't work all the time as I have been. I don't want to work any less." Kayla laughs at her, shaking her head.

"Just a thought." Sheila hugs her tightly to her as they settle in and watch the news together. Both of them so tired that the only thing that's going to complete them at this moment is falling asleep in each other's arms.

# Chapter Fourteen

Sheila wakes up before Kayla does the next morning. Alex is already walking into the bedroom. She can't believe that Alex would be that early in the morning.

"What are you doing up so early?" Sheila asks getting out of bed to see what the matter is as the alarm in the bedroom goes off.

"We have a few weeks before school starts. I just want to make sure that I'm ready for it." He grins assuring her that there's nothing the matter.

Kayla gets up and hits the alarm clock. Then she makes her way to the bathroom. Sheila likes the routine of seeing both them up at the same time.

"Sometimes I come in here when it's school time just to make sure Mom's up." Alex points out before leaving the bedroom.

Sheila gets her housecoat and heads downstairs to make the morning coffee and feeds Alex as he sits at the kitchen table.

"I'm going to have to get used to this routine too. Do you take the bus, do you walk?" Sheila asks him as she makes him a bowl of cereal and pushes it his way.

"No, Mom usually takes me to school." He shrugs his shoulders.

"I can do that. I don't mind doing it." Sheila offers her services.

"I think that Mom would like that too." He laughs at her, shaking his head seeing how happy she is first thing in the morning.

She grabs a bowl of cereal for herself and sits down beside him. They clank their spoons together before they dig into their food.

"Did you hear the schedule for football yet?" Alex asks her, testing to see how serious his mom is about it.

"Yes. I am well aware of what time practice starts and when it ends. What time the games are, even the away games. The coach also has my number if they can't get a hold of your mother." Sheila points out to him.

"Good, that's the same way it is at Linda's at least with the school. I can't wait to tell Dad that I'm going to be joining the football team." His eyes shine as he looks at Sheila.

"Let me guess. He already knows." Alex sighs, rolling his eyes.

"Your mother is just happy that you want to do things. She called them last night to let them know even before you knew." Sheila laughs a little.

Alex nods his head as he finishes eating his cereal. He has to give his mother credit. At least she didn't cry over the fact that Alex didn't want to stay home all the time anymore. He's growing up. If she does cry about it, it's not in front of him.

"I would say that we've gotten a lot closer. It's all right." He shrugs his shoulders, finishing his cereal and drinking down his milk.

"She just loves you very, very, much. You have to remember that no matter what." She tells him taking care of her bowl and his.

Sheila hears the coffee beeping . Before she can make it, Kayla walks into the room and grabs her own cup.

"Good morning." She kisses Alex on the head, kisses Sheila quickly on the mouth and makes her way to the coffee pot.

Sheila grins at her, shaking her head.

"What?" Kayla asks.

"This is how I always hoped it would be with someone someday. I never thought it would come true that my life would turn out like this. That one day two people would come into my life who mean the world to me and I'd be so happy." Sheila explains.

"I'm going to go upstairs and read a book or something." Alex rolls his eyes, but there's a grin on his face before he even leaves the kitchen.

"I know. It's amazing, isn't it?" Kayla laughs when Alex leaves the room.

"More than amazing. It's everything that I ever hoped for," Sheila whispers to her.  Kayla moves away from her.

"I'm not going to be able to work if you keep talking to me like that." She giggles, making her way out of the kitchen and back up the stairs.

Sheila sits down on the counter and shakes her head. She can't stop smiling. They're turning into a family and all she wants is the three of them to be as happy as they are right now.

Throughout the day, Sheila and Alex pass the ball back and forth. She is happy to see that he wants her to be the one that throws it. Even if Kayla was free, Alex knows that she can't throw as far as Sheila can. If he's going to stay on the team, he has to give the coach a reason to keep him in one spot instead of numerous spots.

"What would you be doing right now?" Sheila asks, looking at the clock when they go in for lunch.

"We'd be going out for recess. We have recess closer to the end of the day. We usually have lunch around ten-thirty." He points out to her.

"That's early." She shakes her head, seeing that Kayla hasn't made an appearance yet.

"You make us something to eat. I'm going to go see if your mother's hungry," Sheila tells him, running a hand through his hair as she leaves the kitchen.

She races up the stairs to the office. She sees that the door is open. There's Kayla talking to someone on the headset.

Kayla is looking at the time. She sounds rushed as Sheila shuts the office door and locks it.

Going closer and closer to Kayla, she's not sure that Kayla notices her. She stands behind her, kissing the back of her neck.

Sheila bites down on her lip, closing her eyes as she feels Kayla's hand running up and down the front of her new shirt.

She leans back in the chair, taking the headset off, letting the client continue talking on the phone.

"You know that you've skipped lunch. That's part of your schedule." Sheila whispers against her ear, undoing the buttons of her shirt.

"I'm not really hungry." Kayla gasps when she feels Sheila's hands slipping into the front of her bra. Kayla feels her fingers squeeze her breasts gently.

"No, but I am," she moans to her, taking her hands out of her bra and spinning the chair around so that Kayla's facing her.

"What are you going to do about that?" She asks, raising one of her eyebrows and biting back a smile.

"Mm. I'm going to have a feast." Sheila giggles at her, pulling the skirt that Kayla's wearing up over her legs and her hips.

She moans when she sees that Kayla's not wearing any panties under the skirt and Kayla spreads her legs slowly when she notices Sheila staring at her mound.

Kayla's eyes go to the office door that's shut.

"I've locked it." Sheila moans and shoves her face between Kayla's legs. Kayla spreads her legs wider when she feels Sheila's tongue teasing her, feeling how wet it is, pressing her bud between her lips.

"You know how to please a woman. You know how to make me feel wanted." Kayla moans to her, running a hand through her hair.

"That's all part of my charm," Sheila whispers, her hot breath teasing her bud and making it harder for her.

"Damn," Kayla whispers, pressing her head back against the office chair while Sheila slips a finger inside of her.

She feels Sheila's finger slipping in and out of her faster and faster, loving the wet noise that's coming from her.

"Lick it," Kayla murmurs to her. Sheila gladly removes her finger and slips her tongue into her.

Sheila closes her eyes, tasting the sweetness that she's been craving for a few hours now knowing that regular food wasn't going to hit the spot.

"Just like that. God, I love that. Flick your tongue," Kayla moans to her, tugging on Sheila's hair as she grinds against her mouth.

Sheila continues to flick her tongue back and forth against the spot that Kayla is talking about. Kayla continues to grind faster and faster, trying not to be too loud. She bites down hard on her lip as she feels her legs shaking.

Sheila brings her hands to Kayla's knees and spreads her legs wider so that she can get her tongue inside of her deeper.

"Yes, you make it so hard to work. You make me feel so naughty." Kayla whispers to her, her eyes opening wide each time that Sheila finds that spot with her tongue.

She can't help herself. Her body gives into Sheila's want quickly. She watches as Sheila drinks down the juice that's coming from her hole.

Sheila's greedy while she licked it out, dipping her tongue in and out slowly so that the juice flows over her tongue and down her throat.

Kayla digs her nails into Sheila's shoulders. She tries to grind against her face even harder, but Sheila has her right where she wants her and doesn't stop teasing her until there's nothing left for Kayla to give to her.

"Damn. That lunch was so good." Sheila moans, pulling her skirt back down and standing up on her feet.

"You should give me something to eat too." Kayla licks her lips.

"Can't you have your client waiting for you." Sheila giggles at her, pointing at the headset that's sitting on the desk.

Kayla's eyes grow wide, almost forgetting about the client that she was still talking to herself as Sheila laughs, unlocking the door and heading out of the room closing the door behind her.

Alex is in his room watching television instead of downstairs. He looks tired . She waves to him as she passes his room.

He smiles at her and continues watching the television.

Sheila knows it's okay to have a little downtime without doing anything, without talking to anyone. Everyone needs it every now and again including Alex.

She goes down the stairs, out to the kitchen and opens the backdoor. Putting on her fall jacket, she shuts the door behind her and heads for the woods.

Sheila remembers how they had first started out. Alex running ahead of her, not wanting to wait for her but listened to her when she hollered out to him.

Getting to the clearing she laughs when she sees the pile of leaves that had been scattered around by the wind.

They look sad wondering when they're going to be jumped in again. She continues to walk out to the field and sits down on the boulder.

The sky is getting gray as the leaves pick up because of the breeze. She knows that soon it's going to start snowing.

It won't for a couple of months, but the leaves are going to be buried under all the snow . She's not looking forward to it at all.

That's when she lifts her head and sees that Kayla is there waiting for her at the trail. Sheila stands up on the boulder and waves her over to where she is.

Slowly Kayla makes her way to her and when she's just a few feet away Kayla can see that something's the matter with her.

"You look so sad," Kayla tells her as Sheila holds out her hands for Kayla to take to get onto the boulder with her.

"I wouldn't say sad." Sheila shakes her head, but the smile that she gives doesn't quite reach her eyes.

# Chapter Fifteen

Sheila sits there and looks at the clouds while Kayla holds her hand waiting for her to speak. Waiting for her to say something, anything.

"I come to you with a lot of things. Alex does too." Kayla points out to her.

"It's I just don't want fall to turn to winter. It's a big deal to me. I know that it happens every year, but that takes away a lot of the things that you can do outside." She points out to Kayla, leaning her head against her shoulder.

"That's what's bothering you?" Kayla asks, trying not to smile at the fact that it's such a small thing to be sad about.

"Yeah, in the spring you see the buds on the trees. Before you know it there are new leaves. There are bushes of flowers. In the summertime, we seem to neglect the fact of taking just a second to admire the beauty that's there. Like it's going to be there forever." She sighs.

"The sky is telling me that it's about to rain, not that it's about to snow. Besides, in the winter we go sledding, we go to the winter fests around here. There are so many things to do even if you don't want to be out. Sometimes I have to push myself to do things in the winter. If it weren't for Alex, I would be home all the time and not want to go anywhere when that first snowflake hits." She laughs.

"There's a lot of things changing, for the good. I have to admit that. I can't wait for winter to be over and it hasn't even started yet." She lifts her head and continues to stare at the sky.

She feels a sprinkle hit her nose. She knows that Kayla's right, it's about to rain. The darkening clouds are telling her that she should be heading back home.

"I think that we will find so many things to do in the winter that you're not going to be sad at all about it. That you might feel differently when the snow is melting and leaving." Kayla tells her, sliding off the boulder and putting her feet in the leaves, letting the dead leaves crunch under her feet.

"Where are you going?" Sheila asks her.

"Back toward the house, I don't want to get caught in the rain. Let's go," she tells her, watching as Sheila gets down herself.

She takes Kayla's offered hand as they stroll slowly toward the trail. She feels how warm Kayla's hand is and hopes that it's the same way when the snow does start to fall.

Alex is waiting for them in the kitchen when they come walking through the door. He has his coat on.

"Where are you going?" Sheila asks him.

"Well, Mom wasn't in her office and you weren't around here. So, I was going to go out looking for you, wondering when you guys were going to be home," Alex tells her.

Sheila loves the idea that Alex calls their home hers too. She hugs him to her tightly as if she doesn't ever want to let go.

"Okay, just a little too tight." He fake chokes. Sheila laughs at him before letting him go.

"You do know that I don't want you leaving the house by yourself," Kayla tells him, getting a cup from the cupboard and getting a glass of milk.

"I know that. I know exactly where you guys were. It's not like I'm going to get lost on the trail," he points out to her.

"I thought that you were going to continue working." Sheila looks at Kayla.

"I took half the day off after speaking to that client I just had to. She was going on and on about how things weren't exactly the way she wanted them. I mean, I did what she wanted last week right down to the letter. changed it up on me. That's not my fault." Kayla explains to her.

"You win some. You lose some. You can't beat yourself up over it." Sheila tells her, giving her a supportive hug.

"That's why I'm taking the rest of the day off. I'm not going to work aggravated. I'm not going to get anything done that way and my family doesn't need the stress when I come out of the office." She smiles at Sheila and Alex.

"Every day, you're learning more and more." Sheila winks at her when she lets her go.

"That means that we can play a game, do a puzzle, or something." Alex sounds bored.

"What exactly do you want to do?" Kayla asks when she looks out the window. She sees the rain pelting down on the glass.

"We can bake cookies. That's not too hard to do. Sheila and I can shape them, and you can put them in the oven."

He shrugs his shoulders.

Alex wants to do the things that they used to do with his dad. That was one of them that he missed.

"That sounds like a great idea." Sheila nods her head, going to the baking cupboard and taking out the things that they need along with a mixing bowl.

Alex gets the milk from the counter and the cookie sheets from under the oven and closes the drawer when he places it all on the table.

"I think so too. It's making me hungry already." Kayla tells him, watching the two of them get to work while she turns the oven on.

She keeps an eye on the windows and sees that the wind is picking up. She hopes that the lights don't go out, but she's not sure with the wind coming in.

"Turn the radio on. I think that we're supposed to have a storm tonight. I don't want to be unprepared if the lights get knocked out." Sheila states, looking over at Kayla.

"You're afraid of the dark?" Alex laughs and turns the radio on.

Kayla smiles at her and mouths the words 'thank you' knowing that Sheila had taken one for the team so that she didn't have to.

"Sometimes I am. I don't like the wind either. Storms make me a little nervous. Like I won't make you take a shower tonight if that wind continues to pick up," Sheila tells him.

He smiles and shakes his head, deep down he hopes that the storm continues because he doesn't feel much like showering and sometimes it's because he's lazy, other times it's because he still can't get the water adjusted to his liking. So, he takes longer out of the shower than in the shower.

Sheila looks back at Kayla and sees the love in her eyes as she leans against the counter. The happiness that's shining through Sheila knows that everything is going to work out for the best. She can feel the love in the room and knows that it's only going to grow stronger every day.

Kayla loves the way Sheila's looking at her. It means that she's not going to leave. There's no way that Sheila's going to leave now. She's not worried about that anymore. She just wants to get through every-day life with Sheila by her side.